A King Production presents…

MVFOL

All I See Is The Money…

Female Hustler

A Novel

JOY DEJA KING

This novel is a work of fiction. Any references to real people, events, establishments, or locales are intended only to give the fiction a sense of reality and authenticity. Other names, characters, and incidents occurring in the work are either the product of the author's imagination or are used fictitiously, as those fictionalized events and incidents that involve real persons. Any character that happens to share the name of a person who is an acquaintance of the author, past or present, is purely coincidental and is in no way intended to be an actual account involving that person.

ISBN 13: 978-0991389032
ISBN 10: 0991389034
Cover concept by Joy Deja King
Cover model: Joy Deja King

Library of Congress Cataloging-in-Publication Data;
A King Production
Female Hustler/by Joy Deja King
For complete Library of Congress Copyright info visit;
www.joydejaking.com
Twitter @joydejaking

A King Production
P.O. Box 912, Collierville, TN 38027

A King Production and the above portrayal logo are trademarks of A King Production LLC

This Book is Dedicated To My:

Family, Readers and Supporters.
I LOVE you guys so much. Please believe that!!

—Joy Deja King

"One week they love you. Next week they hate you. Both weeks I got paid..."

~Rihanna~

A KING PRODUCTION

All I See Is The Money...

Female Hustler

A Novel

JOY DEJA KING

Prologue

Nico Carter

"I don't know what you want me to say. I do care about you—"

"But you're still in love with Precious," Lisa said, cutting me off. "I can't deal with this anymore. You're still holding a torch for a woman that has moved on with her life."

"Of course I have love for Precious. We have history and we share a daughter together, but I want to try and make things work with you."

"Oh really, is it because you know Precious

has no intentions of leaving her husband or is it because of the baby?"

"Why are you doing this?" I shrugged.

"Doing what... having a real conversation with you? I don't want to be your second choice, or for you to settle for me because of a baby. Nobody even knows about me. I'm a secret. You keep our relationship hidden like you're ashamed of me or something."

"I'm not ashamed of you. With the business I'm in and the lifestyle I'm in, I try to keep my personal life private. I don't want to make you a target."

"Whatever. I used to believe your excuses, but my eyes have been opened. I'm a lot wiser now. I've played my position for so long, believing that my loyalty would prove I was worthy of your love, but I'm done."

"Lisa stop. Why are you crying," I said, reaching for her hand, but she pulled away. "I was always upfront with you. I never sold you a dream."

"You're right. I sold myself a dream. More like a fairytale. But when I heard you on the phone with Precious that fairytale died and reality kicked in."

"What phone conversation?" I asked, hoping Lisa was bluffing.

"The one where you told Precious she and Aaliyah were the loves of your life and nothing would change that, not even the baby you were having with me. It was obvious that was the first time you had ever even mentioned my name to her."

"Lisa, it wasn't like that," I said, stroking my hand over my face. "You didn't hear or understand the context of the entire conversation." I shook my head; hating Lisa ever heard any of that. "That conversation was over a week ago, why are you just now saying something?"

"Because there was nothing to say. I needed to hear you say those words. I knew what I had to do and I did it."

"So what, you're deciding you don't want to deal with me anymore? It's too late for that. We're having a baby together. You gonna have to deal with me whether you want to or not."

"That's not true."

"Listen, Lisa. I'm sorry you heard what I said to Precious. I know that had to hurt, but again I think you read too much into that. I do care about you."

"Just save it, Nico. You care about me like a puppy," Lisa said sarcastically.

"I get it. Your feelings are hurt and you don't want to have an intimate relationship with me any longer, I have to respect that. But that doesn't change the fact you're carrying my child and I will be playing an active role in their life so I don't want us to be on bad terms. I want to be here for you and our baby."

"You don't have to worry about that anymore. You're free to pursue Precious and not feel obligated to me."

"It's not an obligation. We made the baby together and we'll take care of our child together."

"Don't you get it, there is no baby."

"Excuse me? Are you saying you lied about being pregnant?"

"No, I was pregnant, but..."

"But what, you had a miscarriage?"

"No I had an abortion."

"You killed my child?"

"No, I aborted mine!"

"That was my child, too."

"Fuck you! Fuck you, Nico! You want to stand there and act like you gave a damn about our baby and me. You're such a hypocrite and a liar."

"You had no right to make a decision like that without discussing it with me."

"I had every right. I heard you on the phone confessing your love to another woman and the child you all share together. Making it seem like our baby and me was some unwanted burden.

Well now you no longer have that burden. Any child I bring into this world deserves better than that."

"You killed my child because of a phone conversation you overheard. You make me sick. I think I actually hate you."

"Now you know how I feel because I hate you too," Lisa spit back with venom in her voice.

"You need to go before you meet the same demise as the baby you murdered."

"No worries, I have no intentions of staying. As a matter of fact, I came to say goodbye. I have no reason to stay in New York."

"You're leaving town?"

"Yes, for good. Like I said, there is nothing here for me. I don't want to be in the same city as you. It would be a constant reminder of all the time I wasted waiting for you," Lisa said, as a single tear trickled down her cheek. "Goodbye, Nico."

I watched with contempt and pain as Lisa walked out the door. I couldn't lie to myself. I almost understood why she chose not to keep our baby. I wasn't in love with Lisa and couldn't see me spending the rest of my life with her. The fucked up part was it had nothing to do with her. Lisa was a good girl, but she was right, my heart still belonged to Precious. But I still hated her for aborting our baby. I guess that made me a selfish man. I wanted Lisa to bless me with another child that I could be a father to, but have her accept that she would never have my heart.

At this moment, it was all insignificant. That chapter was now closed. Lisa was out of my life. In the process, she took our child with her and for that I would never forgive her.

Seven Months Later...

"Look at her, mommy, she is so beautiful," Lisa said, holding her newborn daughter in the hospital.

"She is beautiful," her mother said, nodding her head. "What are you going to name her?"

"Angel. She's my little Angel." Lisa smiled.

"That's a beautiful name and she is an angel," Lisa's mother said, admiring her granddaughter. "Lisa, are you okay?" she asked, noticing her daughter becoming pale with a pain stricken expression on her face.

"I'm getting a headache, but I'll be fine," Lisa said, trying to shake off the discomfort. "Can you hold Angel for a minute. I need to sit up and catch my breath," Lisa said, handing her baby to her mother.

"I would love to." Her mother smiled, gently

rocking Angel.

"I feel a little nauseated," Lisa said, feeling hot.

"Do you want me to get the nurse?"

"No, just get me some water," Lisa said. Before Lisa's mother even had a chance to reach for a bottle of water, her daughter began to vomit. In a matter of seconds Lisa's arms and legs began jerking. Her entire body seemed to be having convulsions."

"Lisa... Lisa... what's the matter baby!" Lisa's mother said, her voice shaking, filled with fear. "Somebody get a doctor!" she screamed out, running to the door and holding her grandbaby close to her chest. "My daughter needs a doctor. She's sick! Somebody help her please!" she pleaded, yelling out as she held the door wide open.

"Ma'am, please step outside," a nurse said, rushing into Lisa's room with a couple of other nurses behind her and the doctor close behind.

Lisa's mother paced back and forth in front of her daughter's room for what seemed like an eternity. "It's gonna be okay, Angel. Your mother will be fine," she kept saying over and over again to her grandbaby. "You know they say babies are healing, and you healing your grandmother's soul right now," she said softly in Angel's ear.

"Ma'am."

"Yes... is my daughter okay?" she asked rushing towards the doctor.

"Ma'am, your daughter was unconscious then her heart stopped."

"What are you saying?" she questioned as her bottom lip began trembling.

"We did everything we could do, but your daughter didn't make it. I'm sorry."

"No! No! She's so young. She's just a baby herself. How did this happen?"

"I'm not sure, but we're going to do an autopsy. It will take a couple of weeks for the results to get back. It could be a placental abruption and amniotic fluid embolism, or a brain aneurysm, we don't know. Again, I'm sorry. Do you want us to contact the father of your granddaughter?" the doctor asked.

Lisa's mother gazed down at Angel, whose eyes were closed as she slept peacefully in her arms. "I don't know who Angel's father is. That information died with my daughter."

"I understand. Again, I'm sorry about your daughter. Let us know if there is anything we can do for you," the doctor said before walking off.

"I just want to see my daughter and tell her goodbye," she said walking into Lisa's room. "My sweet baby girl. You look so peaceful." Lisa's mother rubbed her hand across the side of her face. "Don't you worry. I promise I will take care of Angel. I will give her all the love I know you would have. Rest in peace baby girl."

Chapter One

Butterfly Effect

The butterfly effect suggests that small, unnoticeable causes may contribute to huge, unpredictable effects, which is also known as the chaos theory. This analysis may be viewed one way in scientific terms, but if you flip the coin to the other side, the same rules apply when it comes to the journey of life and Angel Riviera was living proof of that.

Angel's life and the lives of others would forever be altered based on one decision, that at the time it was made, Angel's mother Lisa believed it to be an inconsequential necessity. Lisa died without ever knowing that her choice to tell Nico she had aborted their child, would cause the sort of chaos no one could've predicted or been prepared for. And so the butterfly effect begins.

"Grandma, you said you would give me the money so I can get my cheerleader uniform," Angel said when she walked in the kitchen and sat down at the table.

"I know and I will, baby. It's just taking grandma a little longer than I thought it would."

"Why is that?" Angel huffed.

"I had no idea with the cost of the uniform, shoes, practice gear and other stuff you would need almost $400. It's middle school for heavens sake. I didn't think it would be so expensive."

"But the only reason I even tried out for the squad was because you told me to. Now you don't even have the money for me to join."

"Angel, I told you to tryout because I knew you would make it. I use to see you outside practicing with Taren and you was way better than her and she was co-captain of the team. You would never admit it, but I knew you wanted to tryout. I just gave you the push you needed."

"Maybe, but like I said, what's the point of making the team if I can't join," Angel complained, playing with a napkin.

"Baby girl, don't grandma always come through for you? I told you, I'ma get the money. Have a little faith. Now eat yo' dinner. Wanna keep your weight right so you look cute in your uniform," her grandma teased, putting a hot plate of food on the table for Angel.

Angel smiled back at her grandmother with nothing but love in her eyes. Since the day she was born, her Grandma Eileen was all Angel had. Never knowing her mother or father, Angel's grandmother was her world and vice versa. Although Angel did want to join the cheerleading team it hurt her to heart to see her grandmother struggling to find a way to come up with the money she needed, but that was the story of their lives. Her grandmother worked two sometimes three jobs to make ends meet. They were always just getting by and often not even that. Angel could remember several occasions when the lights had been cut off or her grandmother barely had enough money to put gas in her car to get to work.

Through all the hard times, Angel never remembered her grandmother complaining once. That's why even though she loved practicing with her best friend Taren, she never had any intentions of trying out for the squad because she knew they couldn't afford it, but her grandmother insisted. Now Angel felt guilty that her grandmother was probably begging God for some sort of miracle to come up with the $400 she needed.

"Girl, I'm so excited we're going to be on the cheerleading squad together this year!" Taren beamed, as she sat in front of the mirror brushing her hair and making sexy faces. "Mica and the other girls are cool, but it's nothing like having your best friend to cheer at the games with," Taren continued, oblivious that Angel's mind somewhere else. "Angel, aren't you excited? All the football and basketball players are going to be checking for us. The girls are going to be so jelly!"

Angel was lying on Taren's bed staring up at the ceiling, not paying her friend any attention.

"Angel, are you listening to me?" Taren barked, as she stopped brushing her hair and turned to stare at her friend.

"Ummm, yeah, listening," Angel replied.

"Then what did I say?" Taren smacked, not believing her.

"Honestly, my mind is somewhere else, Taren," Angel admitted.

"Where else could your mind be... I mean what's more important than cheerleading? I mean besides clothes, shoes, makeup and of course Bryce Addison," Taren smiled, referring to her junior high boy crush.

"I don't think I'll be able to do cheerleading," Angel said sadly.

"What are talking about, you already made the team."

"Yeah, but my grandmother doesn't have the money to pay for my uniform and other stuff I'll need."

"Are you serious! What a bummer. There has to be a way," Taren said.

"She said that she would get it, but money is already tight. I feel bad that she even has to stress herself over it."

"Maybe I can ask my dad to give you the money," Taren suggested.

"No way!"

"Why not? You know he has the money. His car dealership business is doing extremely well. Look at this new iPod he just got me," Taren bragged, holding up the sleek blue gadget.

"I'm sure he does but I wouldn't feel right having you go to your father for me, plus my grandmother would have a fit. She always tells me not to accept handouts from anybody. That it's better to be without than to beg and if you want something work for it."

"Please, my mother asks for anything and everything she wants, that's why we don't go without nothing," Taren boasted.

"You're just lucky. You have both your parents. If I had a father with money, who I could just call and ask for anything I wanted, my life would be so much different. But it's just my grandmother and me. Even though we're poor, I still feel lucky to have her. I can't lie, I would love to have a rich father," Angel said.

Angel was always envious that Taren had both her mother and father in her life because she had neither. Even though Taren's parents didn't live together, her father always seemed to provide her with everything she wanted and needed.

Both girls lived in Sunrise, Florida, which was about 40 minutes away from Miami. Taren wasn't rich, but she lived with her mother in a nice townhouse on NW 125th Street, whereas Angel grew up in a small two-bedroom apartment on Sunrise Lakes Blvd in a somewhat rundown neighborhood. They had been best friends since elementary school, but as they were getting older, it was becoming more difficult for Angel to deal with Taren having it all and her having nothing.

"Wait! I have an idea," Taren said with excitement, lying on the bed next to Angel.

"What is it?"

"You know Malinda."

"Yeah, what about her, how can she help?" Angel questioned.

"Well, about a month ago she came to me asking did I want to earn some extra money. Like a few hundred dollars every week but I had to turn her down."

"A few hundred dollars?!" Angel repeated as her eyes widened. "Doing what?"

"All I would have to do was drop off and pick up a package twice a week."

"Are you crazy! Why did you turn her down?"

"Because the drop offs and pickups were on the other side of town. It's closer to where you live and I didn't feel like taking the bus over there twice a week. I mean it's not like I really need the money." Taren shrugged. "But it might be something you can do."

"You think so?" Angel asked, rising up from the bed.

"I don't know if Malinda still needs somebody to do it, but I'll call her now. It's worth a try," Taren said, reaching for her cell phone.

Angel stood up and began pacing the floor in Taren's bedroom. Her mind began racing thinking about how she would be able to buy everything she needed to join the cheerleading squad and take that burden off her grandmother. For the first time, Angel felt that maybe she would have an opportunity to have some sort of control of her destiny instead of always feeling hopeless.

Chapter Two

Tables Will Turn

"This is my friend Angel," Malinda said, introducing Angel to her cousin Gavin. Although Angel and Malinda were more like distant school associates than friends that was the angle they agreed to roll with beforehand. Malinda felt her cousin would be more open to give Angel the job if he believed she was someone that was super cool with Malinda, and Angel desperately wanted the gig, so she was willing to follow Malinda's lead. It was a win-win for Malinda. Her cousin gave her a small fee for everybody she recruited and Malinda made Angel promise that if she were able to do it, then she would give her $25 from the money she made.

"So Malinda tells me you wanna put in some work," Gavin said, standing in front of Angel as she sat down on a bench at the park.

"Yeah I do," Angel replied, glancing over at Malinda nervously.

"That's right, cuz, my girl ready to put in that work," Malinda chimed in enthusiastically.

"Malinda, chill. I ain't talkin' to you. I'm speakin' to yo' friend," Gavin spit. "You seem a lil' nervous over there. You ain't scared is you?" he asked Angel.

"No," she lied. Angel swallowed hard trying to keep her composure. Gavin was an intimidating figure. He stood well over six feet tall and had a solid build. Although it was a warm sunny day, Gavin was dressed in all black with a long sleeve shirt and jeans. He was smoking a Newport and spoke in a deep raspy tone that made Angel uneasy.

"How old are you?" he wanted to know.

"I just turned 14."

"I told you she was the right age," Malinda jumped in and said. Gavin shot her a look to shut the fuck up and she quickly did.

"I'm sure Malinda gave you a breakdown on what I would need for you to do." Angel nodded her head yes. "It's 250 a pop and I need you to do it twice a week."

"So $500 for the week?" Angel wanted to make sure she was hearing Gavin correctly. She was under the impression it was going to be around 200 for the week not double that.

"Yeah that's what 250 a pop totals if you doing this twice a week. Why? You want more?" he asked looking over at Malinda.

"No 500 is fine," Angel said with the quickness. "But umm, I'll only need to do it for a week," Angel added, not the two weeks she initially thought.

"I'm not following you," Gavin said, frowning his face. He caught Malinda about to say something, but before she could fully open her mouth, Gavin shot her another glare that instantly put that to an end.

"The thing is..." Angel hesitated.

"The thing is what?" Gavin pressed.

"The thing is, I'm only doing this to raise the money I need to participate in cheerleading at my school. With $500 I'll have what I need," Angel explained.

Gavin got real quiet and Angel regretted divulging that information to him. But she felt it was better to let him know from the jump that this was a short-term gig for her.

Gavin took one more pull from his cigarette and tossed it down on the concrete. "I tell you what. You do this drop off for me tomorrow and another at the end of the week. If you wanna stop after that, then our business will be done."

"That works, but after I do these two times I'll be done. Like I said, I just need the money for cheerleading," Angel said without hesitation.

"Got you." Gavin smiled, which surprised Angel. "Meet me here tomorrow when you get out of school. I'll tell you exactly what to do then. We clear?"

"I'll be here," Angel said, ready to jump up and down from excitement.

"Cool, see you then. I'll talk to you later Malinda," Gavin said before walking to his black Escalade and driving off.

"Yes!" Angel screamed out after Gavin left.

"Yes, is right," Malinda said hi-fiving Angel. "Girl, I thought you had fucked things up for us a couple times, especially when you said you would only do it twice. I guess Gavin decided to take what he could get."

"Yeah, I got worried a few times myself. But I was wondering why did you make that comment about me being the right age?" Angel inquired.

"I've been doing the drops for awhile now, but Gavin came to me asking if I had any friends that needed to make some money. He said things were picking up and he needed more help. But he said they had to be females and under the age of 16."

"Really, why is that?"

"He said the police wouldn't be checking for them like that."

"Police!? Why would he be worried about the police getting involved?"

"Listen, I don't ask my cousin no questions when it comes to his business. As long as I'm getting that cash," Malinda said, rubbing her fingers together, "then I'm straight. So what, you don't want to do it now? If not, then let me know now so I can tell my cousin you out."

Angel knew in her gut what she was about to participate in was shady, but she didn't want to pass on the easy money. She figured if Malinda had been doing it and everything went smoothly then she could do it too. "I don't want out, besides it's only a couple of times. I can do that," Angel reasoned.

"Cool. So tomorrow after school we can come here together because I have to do a drop off too.

"Works for me. Cheerleading squad here I

come!" Angel beamed, before leaving the park with Malinda.

"Girl, what is up? You been missing this last week," Taren said when she ran into Angel in the hallway at school.

"Between studying, putting in that work for Malinda's cousin and helping my grandmother with some things, I've spent the rest of my time sleeping," Angel grumbled.

"How did that go... you know with Malinda's cousin?"

"It was straight. I did the last one yesterday."

"Did he pay you?"

"Yep, he paid in full."

"Wow! I sorta thought Malinda might've been bullshitting, but you actually got paid," Taren said shocked.

"Sure did. I'm actually on my way to pay my cheerleading fees now," Angel said proudly.

"Good for you. But listen, Tony is having a party Saturday night. All the cool people will be there including Bryce Addison. I want you to come with me."

"I can't."

"Why not?"

"For one I have nothing to wear."

"You can burrow something of mine," Taren offered.

"Thanks but that's okay," Angel said, irritated by Taren's suggestion. She knew her friend meant well, but Angel was sick of Taren always offering to let her wear her clothes, especially when it was the outfits that she no longer liked because they weren't hot. It made Angel feel like an unwanted stepchild.

"I have plenty of clothes you can wear. Some of them still have the tags on it."

"Yeah, and they're probably out of style by now," Angel said rolling her eyes. "It's not just the outfit. My hair is a mess. It's been in this French braid all week and I can't afford to go to the salon for a wash and curl."

"I'm going to get my hair done tomorrow. When my dad stops by I can have him give me some extra money so I can pay for you to get your hair done too."

"Taren, why are you so pressed for me to go to this party with you? You've never offered to pay to get my hair done before," Angel questioned.

"Because I've never wanted to go to a party this badly. Bryce rarely goes out and he is going to be there for sure because Tony is his best friend."

"Go with Malinda, or one of the other girls on the squad."

"I don't want to go with them. They get so jealous because all the boys always want to talk to me. I won't be in the mood for that Saturday," Taren said flipping her ponytail. "Pleasssssssse, Angel," she begged.

"Fine."

"Great! So meet me at my house after school so I can give you something to wear."

"I'll buy my own outfit," Angel snapped.

"How? You don't have any money." Taren laughed.

"Don't worry about it. I got this," Angel said and walked off. At that moment Angel decided she would no longer allow Taren to make her feel like she was Cinderella and Angel the dusty stepsister. And she knew exactly how to make it happen.

"Malinda, hold up!" Angel yelled out when she spotted her crossing the street after school. Malinda stopped and waited as Angel ran towards her.

"What's up?" Malinda said when Angel

finally got to her. She gave her a second because Angel was still out of breath from running so fast.

"Listen, I was wondering if I could put some more work in for your cousin."

"I thought you said you were two and done. That all you wanted was to make your lil' cheerleading money and you was good," Malinda mocked.

"I know what I said, but some other expenses have come up and I need to make some more money," Angel said not feeling Malinda's snippy attitude.

"Well, Gavin might not want to fuck with you no more. He don't need no wishy washy people working for him."

"Can I at least ask him myself?"

"I suppose. I'm on way to meet him now. You can come with me. But if he shuts you down, don't say I didn't warn you," Malinda stated.

"No problem. Just take me to your cousin... thanks," Angel said, trying her hardest not to let the tone of her voice reveal how aggravated she was with Malinda. Angel was on a mission to change her circumstances for the better and she wasn't going to let Malinda or anyone else stop her.

Chapter Three

Spend A Little Dough

When Angel and Malinda finally got to the spot to meet Gavin, they had to wait for over an hour before he finally arrived.

"Damn, Gavin, you stop being able to tell time," Malinda snapped, furious her cousin had them waiting for so long.

"Yo chill. I've had a fucked up day and your mouth is not what I'm here for."

"I ain't here for you to have me sitting outside in this hot ass sun waiting for you to show up. If you had been here on time, you wouldn't have to hear my mouth," Malinda spit back, not letting up.

"You just like yo' mother, don't never know when to shut the fuck up," Gavin said shaking his head.

"Yeah my mother and yo' aunt. Maybe she need to know that you want her to shut the fuck up," Malinda folded her arms and said in a threatening voice.

"I don't give a fuck what you tell Aunt Janay. As a matter of fact, you can take yo' silly ass on now and tell her. Angel here can make yo' drop today and make yo' money," Gavin told Malinda.

Malinda stared at Gavin then glanced over at Angel. "What you mean she can make my drop today?"

"You heard me. Like I said, you don't know when to shut the fuck up. But maybe missing out on making a little dough will help you to remember next time."

"Fuck you, Gavin!" Malinda shouted. Angel stood there not saying a word as Malinda stormed off.

"You got something you wanna say?" Gavin questioned Angel in his normal intimidating grumpy tone, but she was unbothered. Angel only had making money on her mind and if that meant tolerating Gavin's less than charming demeanor, she was willing to do so.

"No, I'm good," she replied.

"I'm assuming since you showed up with Malinda today, that means you want me to put you back to work."

"I do."

"What happened to that two and done?"

"Life happened," Angel said.

"What you mean by that?" Gavin asked as if taken back by Angel's comment.

"What I mean is that I want a better life than what I have now. Maybe better is the wrong word," she said looking down.

"Nah, ain't nothing wrong with better."

"I'm tired of watching my grandmother struggle. I'm tired of being without. I'm tired of feeling less than because our basic needs can barely be met," Angel admitted, holding back tears.

"I tell you what little girl. You work for me and follow my lead, you'll have more than enough to have all yo' needs met and leftovers. I promise. I'll teach you everything you need to know to get paid in full."

"Fo' real?" Angel questioned, surprised by Gavin's promise.

"Fo' real. But I ain't gon' tolerate all that slick

talkin' like my cousin be doing. You not gonna learn shit from me wit' that type of mouth. You dig?"

"I dig," Angel said, nodding her head. "All I want is to be able to help my grandmother and be able to afford to buy a few nice things for myself. If I have to keep my mouth shut, listen, and learn from you in order to make that happen, then that's what I'll do," she agreed. Angel was learning at a young age the importance of being willing to play your position to get what you wanted.

"Good, now go drop off that package for me."

"Okay, I'm on it," Angel said picking up her backpack so she could go.

"Angel, wait a minute," Gavin called out. Angel stopped in her tracks and turned around. "Here, take this," he said holding out his hand.

"This is way too much," Angel said shaking her head. She had never seen that much money at one time. "What is this for?"

"It's for you. Let's just say it's a little advance on all the money I know you gon' make me once I teach you what you need to know. After you put in your work, go get yourself something nice." Gavin smiled

It was the first time Angel had ever seen Gavin not mean mugging. She didn't know how to react, mainly because she was so stunned. She had more than enough money to get her hair done, buy an outfit for the party, get her grandmother something nice and help her with a few bills. Earlier today, Angel felt hopeless like her life would be filled with misery, but within a matter of seconds all that changed. When Gavin put all that cash in the palm of Angel's hand, she vowed never to be broke again.

Angel spent her Saturday ripping through Sawgrass Mills outlet mall. She was like a kid in a candy store filled with all her favorite treats. This was the first time she could ever afford to buy something from one of the stores. Normally, Angel's grandmother would get her clothes from either the Salvation Army or thrift shops. Of course, sometimes Taren would give Angel some of her old clothes, but most of the time they didn't fit because by the time Taren had passed them down to her, they had outgrown them.

No more of Taren's hand me downs or thrift shops for me. Nope, for now on I'll be able to have new clothes that actually have tags, Angel thought to herself when she walked into BeBe admiring an outfit she saw in the stores window.

"This will be perfect for the party." Angel grinned taking it off the rack. "Tonight is going to be amazing," Angel said on her way into the dressing room, without a care in the world.

"Where have you been all day and what's in those bags?" Grandma Eileen asked when Angel got home. "And your hair. You got your hair done. You look beautiful just like your mother."

"Grandma, your eyes are watering up."

"Don't mind me, I'm just getting a little sentimental looking at you. Sometimes I forget you're the spitting image of your mother, especially with your hair like that. Enough of that reminiscing, where you been, Angel?"

"I told you about the party I'm going to tonight. I got my hair done and bought a few things. I got you something too, Grandma. You're going to look so pretty in this dress," Angel beamed pulling out a long pink maxi dress from a shopping bag.

"Omigoodness, this is for me, Angel? It's

gorgeous!" she beamed, putting it up to her chest. "Child, I can't keep this. I can't believe you spent that much money on a dress!" Grandma Eileen gasped looking at the price tag. "Where is all this stuff coming from? First you tell me you were able to raise the money to join the cheerleading squad, now this. What is going on, Angel?"

"Grandma, I didn't want to tell you this because I knew you would be a little upset but please don't be mad," Angel pleaded.

"Just tell me, Angel."

"Taren went to her father to help me out and he agreed."

"Oh hell no! And you spent the money on clothes. You taking all this shit back," Grandma Eileen yelled, throwing the pink maxi dress back in the shopping bag.

"I earned that money. He gave me like an advance on my paycheck for work."

"Work... what sort of work are you doing?" she asked suspiciously.

"Every day after cheerleading practice I've been going to his car dealership and answering phones, cleaning up. Basically being everybody's slave. But it's good money and like I said he gave me an advance."

"Why did he give you an advance?"

"So I could pay my cheerleading cost and

have some extra money leftover to buy myself something nice and you too. Also, to help you out a little," Angel said, placing some money on the living room table.

Grandma Eileen stared at her granddaughter with apprehension. She wasn't completely buying Angel's story, but at the same time it could've been all true. Taren was always bragging about how much money her father had and that business was good for him so it was possible that Angel was working for him. Although she did feel a little guilty, Grandma Eileen felt somewhat elated that not only did Angel give her some financial help, but also she couldn't remember the last time she had a new dress. It was a combination of all those things that made her want to believe her granddaughter was telling her the truth.

"I hope you're not lying to me, Angel."

"I'm not. You always told me never to take handouts and work for what I want. That's all I'm doing. Please let me."

"Okay, baby girl, you can keep working, but don't let your grades slip or you'll have to quit," she cautioned.

"I understand. I'll be able to juggle both. Thank you," Angel said giving her grandma a hug.

"You're welcome, and thank you. The dress is beautiful and I truly appreciate you helping me out with the extra money," she sniffled, rubbing Angel's back. Grandma Eileen meant every word. She didn't want to worry Angel, but her hours had got cut at her second job and she was short this month for bills. The extra money came right when they needed it and she felt once again God was answering her prayers, this time through her beloved granddaughter.

Chapter Four

Mean Girls

"I thought you were supposed to be coming with Angel," Mica commented as she and a couple of other girls stood in a circle talking to Taren.

"She'll be here soon. She was running late so I told her I would meet her at the party," Taren replied, looking over Mica's shoulder to get a look at Bryce. He was standing in a corner talking to Tony and another guy. He hadn't said a word to Taren since she got there and she was trying to think of a way to get his attention without appearing thirsty.

"This party is kinda boring," Mica complained to the group of girls, sipping on her punch.

"Yeah, it is a little slow. All the guys are standing together and all the girls are together. Ain't no co-mingling going on," another girl named Patrice said, adding her two cents.

"Maybe we need to start dancing to the music," Taren suggested, thinking some sexy moves would make Bryce take notice.

"Dance with who, each other?" Mica sulked.

"Yeah, what's wrong with that?" Taren spat, tired of listening to Mica and the other girls be so negative. She was ready to make a beeline over to Bryce, but decided to wait for Angel to arrive for that much needed girl support.

"Girl, there are too many cute boys in this party to be dancing with one of you. And check out Bryce Addison, he is the cutest of them all." Mica smirked, turning around so she was facing his direction.

Taren was ready to knock the shit out of Mica for lusting after Bryce. She knew he wasn't her boyfriend yet, but trust Taren was plotting on it and she didn't want any interference.

Finally, Angel is here. I can get away from these losers and have some fun, Taren thought when she saw Angel coming through the front door.

"Is that Angel?" Patrice questioned with a stunned look on her face. The other girls turned around to see.

"Yeah that's her," Taren answered.

"Wow, she looks really pretty," one of the other girls standing with them said.

"She sure does," Patrice mumbled, with an attitude. Patrice, Mica and the other girls were all glaring at Angel as if she was unwanted competition. Taren thought her best friend looked great and found it hilarious that the other girls couldn't hide their jealousy, that was until she witnessed Bryce leave his friends to stop and talk to Angel.

"Look at her! She's flirting with my man," Mica grumbled to the other girls.

"I didn't know you and Bryce were dating," Taren said sarcastically.

"Everybody knows that I like him," Mica snarled.

"A lot of girls like Bryce, but it means nothing if he doesn't like you back," Taren reminded her.

Instead of responding, Mica ignored Taren's remark and focused her attention back on Angel who was still talking to Bryce. They were laughing and seemed to be enjoying each other's company, which was driving not only Mica crazy, but Taren too. Besides Angel nobody else was aware that she also had a crush on Bryce and she wanted to keep it that way for now. But it was making Taren cringe that he hadn't shown her an ounce of interest the entire time she had been at the party, but the moment Angel walked through the door he couldn't stay away.

"Excuse me, girls. I need to go get Angel," Taren said, rushing past them. She heard one of them call her name, but acted as if she didn't. Taren had no desire to stay in that circle, plus she thought her best friend and boy crush were getting a little too cozy. "Angel, hi! You look beautiful," Taren smiled, giving her a hug.

"Thanks! So do you. Bryce, this is my friend Taren I was telling you about," Angel said, winking at Taren when he wasn't looking.

"I was telling Angel about this arcade I like to go to and she was saying how you're into playing video games."

"Yeah, totally," Taren lied. She had absolutely no interest in video games, but Taren had no problem pretending she did if it could get her closer to Bryce.

"Cool, maybe we can all go together," Bryce, said.

"That would be awesome." Taren smiled.

"So when do you want to go, Angel? I'm sure Tony is down for going. You can hang out with him, Taren. He's into video games too."

Taren's mouth dropped. She was hoping Bryce was interested in her. She had no idea he was trying to toss her off to his friend Tony. Taren was mortified.

"Let me think about it. I have a lot going on right now," Angel finally said.

"Okay, but can you give me your phone number so I can call you."

"I can't. I have a boyfriend."

"You do? Does he go to our school?"

"No he doesn't, but he wouldn't be cool with us talking on the phone."

"I understand. If you change your mind, let me know. Nice meeting you, Taren," Bryce said then walked back over to where his friends were.

"Why did you lie and tell him you have a boyfriend? I hope it wasn't because of me," Taren sighed.

"I would never give Bryce my phone number knowing you like him."

"It doesn't matter. Clearly he's not interested in me, he wants to talk to you. I say go for it."

"Taren, you don't mean that. You like him and you never know, he might end up liking you too."

"I doubt it."

"Doubt what?" Mica asked, sneaking up behind Angel and Taren.

"Nothing that concerns you, Mica," Taren said, rolling her eyes.

"So what's up with you and Bryce, Angel?"

"There is nothing up, Mica."

"You all seemed awfully chummy."

"We were having a conversation, nothing more."

"Hmmm, if you say so. I see you finally got your hair done and got some decent clothes. Or did Taren let you borrow that outfit?"

"Shouldn't you be somewhere practicing your cheers? You are the captain and it never looks good for the leader of the team to constantly fuck up routines during practice," Angel sniped.

"You come into this party with your fancy new outfit, your hair did and now you think you're hot shit because Bryce Addison showed interest in you. Get over yourself and don't forget I am the captain of the squad and you're just one of the members."

"Mica, chill. Stop giving Angel a hard time because Bryce wants her and not you. That's so not cool," Taren said, before taking Angel's hand so they could walk away.

"The look on Mica's face when you said that was priceless." Angel laughed.

"Wasn't it? She irks me anyway. Come on let's get some punch," Taren said. "And, Angel..."

"Yeah."

"If you want to talk to Bryce I'm totally cool with it. I don't want you thinking I'm a psycho like Mica."

"You're def not like Mica and there are a ton of guys out here, one that my best friend hasn't been crushing on forever. So I'm good."

"You have to admit, he is a cutie though," Taren gushed.

"Yeah, he is." They giggled.

Taren and Angel spent the rest of the night clowning Mica and Taren making googly eyes at Bryce. Although Angel had been reluctant, she was glad she decided to come to the party and more than that she was happy Taren didn't let Bryce's interest in her ruin their night.

"Okay everybody get in position," Mica said clapping her hands. "Let's practice this routine one more time and we're aiming for perfection. Angel, you're going to be the flyer on this move. Patrice and Lawanda, you'll spot her," Mica directed. "Is everybody ready?"

"Yes!" the girls replied enthusiastically. All

the girls got into position and began doing their routine. They were cheering as if it was an actual halftime show. Angel had a strong core, a good sense of balance and was extremely flexible which made her an excellent flyer and more successful with her stunts. Angel prepared herself for her flip. She controlled her weight by keeping her abdominal muscles tight so she could stabilize her spinal column while in the air. She used her shoulders and upper body to pull her weight off the base beneath her. Angel locked out her legs so they would stay tight. She didn't want to risk becoming off balance and falling. Even at 14, Angel was almost a pro at staying focused and steady. So when she landed harshly on her ankle on the gym floor it was no accident.

"Oooooch!" she screamed out in excruciating pain.

"Angel, are you okay?!" Taren hollered, running over to her.

"No, I think I broke my ankle. It hurts so bad," Angel cried.

"What are you all standing around here for, get some help!" Taren yelled. She noticed Mica, Patrice, and Lawanda huddled together snickering. "Did you all do this on purpose... answer me?" Taren demanded to know, walking up on the three girls.

"Taren, what are you talking about. We didn't do anything. I guess Angel isn't as good a flyer as we all thought. She couldn't hold her balance and fell," Patrice snapped.

"From where I was standing that looks like what happened to me too. Maybe Angel should take the advice she gave me and practice more." Mica gave Taren a half smile. "Okay everybody, practice is over for today. I'll see you all back here tomorrow," Mica said not paying Taren or Angel any attention.

Taren realized it was a waste of time trying to get the truth out of Mica and the other girls, but she knew they were lying. She focused her attention back on Angel instead.

"Angel, I'm so sorry this happened to you. I'm going to get you to a doctor. Don't worry, everything will be fine," Taren said trying to console her best friend. "But trust me, they'll get theirs," Taren mumbled under her breath, as she and some of the other girls carried Angel out of the gym.

Chapter Five

The Chase

"I can't believe you're on crutches. How long did the doctor say you'd need them?" Taren asked.

"The good news is it's a second degree sprain which isn't exactly good, but at least it isn't a torn ligament. The doctor said recovery time is anywhere from four to eight weeks."

"Wow, what a bummer."

"I know. No more cheerleading for a while. I went through all that trouble to get the money to join and now I can't even be a part of the team."

"Yeah, because of Mica and her minions. I swear I wish we could prove that Patrice and Lawanda let you fall on purpose so both of them and Mica would be kicked off the squad."

"You know they're not going to admit to any wrongdoing, but guess what I can't stress myself over it. An important lesson I learned from Gavin is that life brings you enough stress so don't worry over things you have no control over," Angel said proudly.

"You learned a lesson from Gavin... who is Gavin?"

"You know Gavin, Malinda's cousin."

"You're learning lessons from Malinda's cousin now? I thought you were done working for him."

"Nope. I decided the money was too good to pass up. Plus, he told me he was going to teach me everything I needed to know so one day I could be a boss just like him."

"A boss!" Taren burst out laughing. "A boss of what? You're 14. The only thing we need to be worried about is keeping ourselves cute, so we can land a boss as our man and he can take care of us. Look how good my mother has it. She doesn't even have to work."

"Taren, that's the difference between me and your mother. I don't want a man to take care of me. I want to take care of myself. I don't even have a father to take care of me. So you better believe I'm not going to rely on a man to do it."

"You were always weird." Taren shrugged, playing with her hair.

"And honestly, I think it's a good thing that I messed up my ankle."

"Why would you say that?" Taren asked, shocked by Angel's statement.

"Because now I can concentrate more on my schoolwork and making money. Cheerleading was holding up my paper chase anyway."

"Where is my friend Angel... please bring her back to me," Taren mocked. "We can finish this conversation later. My dad just texted me, he's outside."

"Tell your dad I said hi."

"I will. He's taking me shopping."

"I swear you go shopping like ever week."

"Because I got it like that. My daddy spoils me and if Bryce doesn't realize I'm the only girl for him then I'll go on the hunt for a new boy who can spoil me just like my daddy does," Taren boasted.

"Girl, you are a mess with a capital M. Call me later on."

"I will. Hope you get off those crutches soon. Love you girly, bye." Taren gave Angel a hug and waved before heading out. Angel glanced out her window, watching Taren get in her dad's Escalade. She thought about how lucky Taren was to have such a close relationship with her father. Angel wished the same for herself, but she knew that was nothing more than a far-fetched fantasy. Angel decided a long time ago the only person she could depend on to make her dreams come true was herself.

Over the last couple months with Angel's grandmother working long hours and no cheerleading practice to keep her occupied, Angel began spending all of her spare time with Gavin. He became her unofficial mentor and she enjoyed every second of it. Gavin took Angel almost everywhere he went. He liked the fact that although Angel was young, she would listen and follow directions without giving him a hard time. She was like a sponge and would soak up every word he said. They had grown extremely close. He began looking at her as not just someone who worked for him but as a little sister.

"So where are we headed today?" Angel

asked Gavin, sitting shotgun in his convertible Mercedes.

"We have to meet with a potential new client of mine in Miami," Gavin informed her.

"We're going to Miami. I've never been there. I know it's basically down the street from us but I've never had a reason or opportunity to go."

"Well sit tight little lady 'cause I'm about to introduce to a whole 'nother world you didn't even know existed."

When Gavin and Angel arrived at the front gate of the breathtaking estate her heart began pounding. There were at least 200 feet of Biscayne Bay frontage and a superb Miami skyline view. The architecture gave her a Spain and Italy feel with arched arcades, covered terraces, open interiors and extensive use of stone and tile.

"This place is amazing. Wait, I don't even think amazing is a cool enough word to describe a house like this," Angel said completely mesmerized.

"Wait 'til you see the inside. Try to keep your cool little lady. Remember what I taught you, people don't know where you been or what you have unless you open your mouth and tell them.

I'm exposing you to another side of life because it's time for you to see what's out here for the taking. You got big dreams, well now they've just gotten bigger," Gavin said and proceeded to drive through the gates.

When they entered the home, Angel put on her poker face as Gavin told her to always do when they were in a place of business. She nodded her head politely and only spoke when spoken to. She sat on the couch across from Gavin and two Mexican men. While the three of them began making small talk, Angel used the time to observe her surroundings. The house seemed to be over 12,000 square feet. A few minutes later, a Mexican woman came in the room and approached her.

"Come with me. I show you around," the woman said, speaking in broken English. Angel turned towards Gavin to see if it was okay for her to go. He nodded his head giving her the go ahead. "Follow me," was all the woman said and the tour of the home seemed to take over an hour. The home appeared to be fully renovated. There was a customized chef's kitchen equipped with stainless steel appliances, a wine cellar with temperature control for bottles. An elevator, integrated security and camera system, Lutron lighting, a private master terrace, custom designed walk-in closets and a service entrance. Outside, the gated entry opened to grounds of more than one acre, encompassing a lush royal palm forest, a koi pond, a huge pool and spa surrounded by Dominican coral stone deck and complimented by a kitchen and cabana. The curved coconut palms led to water's edge that had a large new dock for a boatlift and jetski lift.

"Beautiful," Angel stated sweetly and said nothing else. When she sat back down, they seemed to be having the same small talk they were making before she left. Then about five minutes later the three men shook hands and they left.

Gavin waited until they had gotten into the car and left the estate before speaking. "I told you that crib was sick," he said looking over at Angel.

"You didn't exaggerate."

"They gave me a tour the first time I came too. It's like a tradition for them."

"You can get lost in a house that big. But I wouldn't mind living like that."

"And you will."

"You think so?" Angel questioned.

"I know so. You're special, Angel. If you put your mind to it, there ain't nothing you can't have." All Angel could do was smile. That was the first time besides her grandmother that anyone had told Angel she was special. It meant so much coming from Gavin because she looked up to him.

"Thank you for saying that."

"I mean it. You're a hard worker and you're loyal because of that I'm giving you a raise."

"Are you serious!"

"You know I don't play when it comes to money. Those men we just met with, we came to an agreement. Business will be booming so I'll need you to put in even more work. The raise is my way of showing you how much I appreciate and respect hard work. One day you'll be the boss of your own operation and always remember to look out for your best workers. Without them you can't win, but with them you'll stay at the top. So make sure they are well compensated."

"I will. That's a promise." Angel sat back in the drop top daydreaming about when she would become a boss. Angel never questioned Gavin about what sort of operation he ran, but she was far from naïve. She got a glimpse at all the money he was making and the flashy lifestyle he lived, expensive cars, jewelry, endless cash and a very nice house. Also, the people she had to meet with for her drop offs and pickups. It was a lot for a guy in his early 20s. Angel figured he was dealing drugs, but she reasoned he was a businessman just like any other entrepreneur. In her mind,

Gavin was grinding to live a better life, just like she was striving for and Angel was determined to get there.

Chapter Six

The Promise

"Look at you. You don't even look like the same person anymore," Taren said when her and Angel sat down for lunch in the cafeteria. "You wearing designer clothes, nails done, hair done, you even have on makeup."

"I have on lip gloss and a little mascara. You have on way more makeup than me," Angel said, taking a bite of her pizza.

"Sure, but I've always worn makeup. I guess I'm not used to seeing you so put together. Dare

I say you look more put together than me." Taren sighed.

"What can I say, I'm growing up. I'll be 15 soon you know. Plus, Gavin is always giving me style pointers. He says if you have the appearance of success then success will come to you."

"Gavin... Gavin... Gavin. I rarely get to spend time with you anymore, but when I do, all you talk about is Gavin. It's like you worship him or something."

"Worship isn't the right word, but he's done a lot for me. He's changed my life for the better. He's made me realize that anything is possible."

"If you say so. So what else has been going on with you besides your Gavin obsession?"

"Nothing really. Just schoolwork and work-ing for Gavin."

"I take it that means you have no more interest in cheerleading."

"Hell no. My ankle has been better for awhile now, but I have no desire to put on a cheerleading outfit no time soon."

"Is it because of Mica and the other girls."

"If I really wanted to be back on the squad, I wouldn't let those jealous bitches keep me away."

"Then what is it?"

"I think I can learn more working for Gavin

then doing flips and cartwheels for some silly athletes."

"Well excuse me," Taren said, getting offended.

"Sorry, Taren. I didn't mean to sound negative. Cheerleading is cool it's just not the right fit for me anymore. "But listen, how about we go to the movies tonight. We haven't done that in a long time."

"That would be perfect. I'm having an early dinner with my dad, we can meet up and go to the movies afterwards."

"Sounds like a plan. Now let's finish eating so we can get to class," Angel said taking one last bite of her pizza before the bell rang.

"You'll be delivering to a new customer today. Something happened to the previous person he was getting his product from so I'll be his new supplier. Everything should go smoothly and of course, as always I'll have one of my men keeping tabs from a short distance. But if you have any problems call me," Gavin said handing me the package.

"I got you. I'll be in touch soon."

"Before you go, I got something for you."

"You have something for me… like a gift?" she said puzzled.

"Yeah, silly little lady, a gift," he joked.

"You love calling me little lady."

"'Cause that's what you are. A little lady that sometimes thinks she's a grown woman. But here take this. I hope you like it."

Angel opened the small black velvet box and her eyes got big. "Are these real diamonds?" she said in awe of the shiny sparklers.

"Don't come at me like that. You know I don't do fake shit," Gavin said, with a don't play with me look on his face.

"I'm just so surprised you got these for me. Why would you do something so nice?" Angel asked still staring at the diamond earrings, unable to stop admiring them.

"Showing my appreciation."

"But you already gave me a huge raise."

"I know, but when someone is loyal to you, you have to find different ways to reward them so they stay loyal."

"Gavin, you don't ever have to worry about that. I'll always be loyal to you. Besides my grandmother, no one has ever looked out for me the way you have."

"Are you gon' put them on or just keep looking at me?" Gavin chuckled.

"I guess I should put them on," Angel said nervously, afraid she would drop them because her hands were shaking. She had never seen anything so beautiful before in person and was still wrapping her mind around the fact they belonged to her.

"They look perfect on you."

"Thank you. They're so beautiful. This is the nicest gift anyone has ever given me."

"I'm happy you're pleased. You are turning into such a beautiful young lady. You know you're like a sister to me. I really got love for you."

"I feel the same way about you, Gavin."

"Always remember your worth, Angel. Never let any man make you feel less than. Do you understand?"

"Yes, of course."

"Good, because soon more and more guys are gonna be steppin' to you, some good, most of them bad. Don't fall for the bullshit. A good man can be one of the best things that ever happen to you, a bad one can be the worst. So move with caution and make your decisions using this," Gavin said pointing to his head, "and not this," he then patted his chest where his heart would be. "Got it?"

"Got it."

"Good, now get the hell outta here. You got work to do," Gavin said brushing her off.

On Angel's way to deliver the package to Gavin's new customer, she kept looking in every mirror she came across. The diamonds seemed to light up Angel's entire face. They made her feel like a dainty princess. By the time she reached her destination, Angel had pulled her hair back in a ballerina bun so she could get the full effect of the diamond's decorating her ear.

Angel glanced down at the time on her phone to make sure she wasn't late for the drop off. When she looked up, she was surprised to see a familiar face standing in front of her.

"Mr. Owens, what are you doing here?" Angel stuttered, when she locked eyes with Taren's father.

"I guess I should be asking you the same thing," he replied, looking around as if double-checking that seeing his daughter's friend wasn't some sort of bizarre coincidence.

"I'm delivering something for a friend of mine... and you?"

He hesitated for a second before saying, "I would be the one picking it up."

"Oh. So you know...." Angel paused waiting for Mr. Owen's to finish her sentence because she wanted to make sure that this wasn't a mistake.

"Gavin. Yes, I know Gavin."

"Then this belongs to you," Angel said handing the package to him.

"And I need to give you this," right before handing his envelope to Angel he paused until she looked directly in his face. "I'm sure you know that you understand Taren can never know this meeting took place."

"I won't say a word. I promise."

"Smart girl," Mr. Owens said giving her the envelope. Angel stood in disbelief for 15 minutes after Taren's father left. All this time she thought her best friend's father was a legitimate business owner, but instead he was selling drugs. If Taren ever learned the truth, Angel decided it wouldn't come from her because this was one secret she planned on keeping to herself.

Chapter Seven

Executive Decision

For the next few months, it was difficult for Angel to be around Taren. Whenever she would bring up her father, which was often, it was weird not being able to tell her that she was seeing him every week, sometimes twice a week. Mr. Owens had become a regular customer of Gavin and that meant Angel was seeing him often. The only way Angel was able to keep herself from feeling guilty was by reminding herself, that Gavin always stressed that she wasn't allowed to discuss his customers with anybody. Technically, Mr. Owens was a customer so her dealings with him were off limits. But that still didn't shake the awkward feeling Angel would get every time she was around Taren.

Angel was sitting at her desk in math class thinking about how she was supposed to meet Taren after school and she wasn't looking forward to it. While she debated if she should cancel or not the vibrating of her phone snapped her out of her thoughts. She looked down at her cell and saw it was Gavin calling. Angel found it strange that he would be calling since he knew she was in school and he never called her during this time.

"Mr. Montgomery, can I use the restroom please?" Angel raised her hand and asked. After getting permission, Angel rushed to the bathroom and called Gavin.

"I need to see you," Gavin said before Angel could get even a word out.

"I can't come right now, I'm at school. Is everything okay."

"I'll pick you up after school. I'll be parked out front," Gavin stated and hung up.

That was strange. What is going on with him? He sounded so cold and distant. It must be serious because Gavin has never picked me up from school.

But what could it be? Angel thought to herself as she walked back to class.

For Angel the end of the school day couldn't get there fast enough. When the bell rang, Angel grabbed her belongings and rushed out the classroom. On her way down the hallway she heard someone calling her name. When Angel turned around she saw it was Taren.

"Where are you rushing off to? You were supposed to meet me at my locker, remember?" Taren reminded her.

"I'm so sorry. Something came up and I can't hangout after school today."

"What... why? We were supposed to get our mani/pedi then get something to eat."

"I know, Taren, but I have to meet with Gavin. He's actually waiting for me outside right now."

"Are you serious? I'm so sick of this Gavin guy. You barely have time for me anymore. I'm supposed to be your best friend or have you forgotten that Angel."

"No, I haven't forgotten and you are my best friend. I promise we can go tomorrow and it will be my treat," Angel added.

"I don't need you to treat me to anything," Taren shot back as if repulsed by Angel's offer.

"I've been had money. Remember my father is rich. You're the one who all of a sudden gets a few extra dollars in your pockets and don't know how to act. So spare me. Keep your little money because I don't need it," Taren barked and stormed off.

"Taren, wait!" Angel yelled out, but she kept walking. "I'll call her later. I have to see what's going on with Gavin," Angel said out loud, becoming anxious as she rushed out the school building. Like he said he would, Gavin was parked out front waiting.

"What took you so long?" Gavin asked in an icy tone when Angel got in the car.

"I ran into a friend. She needed to talk to me about something important. Sorry you had to wait. So what's up? You didn't sound like yourself when I spoke to you earlier," Angel said as Gavin drove off.

"You know I had to go out of town so I only had an opportunity to go through the envelopes everybody picked up for the week today."

"Okay, so what's the problem?"

"Open the glove compartment," Gavin directed. Angel did what he said. "Get that envelope and open it up."

"Is this some sort of joke?" Angel said seeing the colorful Monopoly money inside the envelope.

"You tell me."

"I don't understand," Angel said confused.

"That's one of your envelopes that you picked up, Angel."

"Me... this came from me?"

"Yes. Did you steal from me?" Gavin questioned with a stern glare on his face.

"How could you even ask me something like that? I would never steal from you. You're my family," Angel said as her eyes watered up.

Gavin pulled over to the side of the street and put his car in park. "Ronnie said that when he met you, the money he owed me was in the envelope. He said you must've taken it out and switched it with that paper money."

"Who is Ronnie... wait are you talking about Mr. Owens?" Angel questioned not used to hearing Taren's father called by his first name.

"Yes, Ronnie Owens. Now why would that man lie on you? For the last few months I've been doing business with him, we haven't had any problems."

"And I've been working for you for almost a year and I've been nothing but loyal. I can't believe Mr. Owen's would lie on me like that especially when I've been keeping his secret."

"What secret?"

"Mr. Owens is my best friend Taren's dad. The

first time we met he made me promise not to tell her because she thinks he owns a car dealership and other businesses and that's how he makes all his money."

"I see. Why didn't you tell me you knew him?"

"Because I don't know him like that. I've been around him briefly a few times because of Taren. I didn't think it was a big deal to you. I was worried about Taren finding out the truth."

"I see," Gavin said, tapping his fingers on the steering wheel.

"But you have to believe me, Gavin. I put this on everything I didn't open that envelope. I never open your envelopes. I feel it's none of my business. I do what you ask and that's it. All I can guess is that Mr. Owens figured that because of my age you would assume that I was capable of doing something like that. And because he's done good business you would believe him over me. I hope he's not right."

"I believe you, Angel. In my gut, I never thought you stole from me, but I had to be sure. Your most trusted allies can become your most lethal enemies all because of greed. I didn't think that happened to you, but I wanted to be positive," Gavin said, tossing the envelope back in the glove compartment.

"You're so good to me. I would never destroy our friendship over money... never. I hope you never doubt me again."

"I won't. I'ma take you home. Enjoy your day off. Do something nice for yourself," Gavin said, putting a handful of $100 bills in Angel's palm.

"You don't have to give me this," Angel said handing the money back to Gavin.

"No, you take it. I want you to have it. It's my way of apologizing for even doubting you for a second."

"You don't owe me an apology. I'm just glad we're still good. I don't know what I would do if I didn't have you in my life."

"Well you don't have to worry 'cause I ain't going nowhere. Now go buy yourself something nice. I'll see you tomorrow."

"Okay, see you then," Angel said, getting out the car. As Angel walked to her apartment, she kept thinking about what Gavin told her. She couldn't believe Taren's father had stole from him and then tried to place the blame on her. She was tempted to call her best friend right now and tell her the truth about her father, but Angel opted against it.

"Who was that man that just dropped you off?" Angel heard her grandma ask, interrupting her thoughts.

"Grandma, what are you doing here? I thought you had to work."

"I had to stop at home and pick something up before I went in. Now answer my question. Who was that man?"

"He works at my job. I didn't realize they didn't need me to work today so he gave me a ride home so I wouldn't have to catch the bus."

"Oh, well let me get out of here so I won't be late. I left you some food in the oven. You have my number at work. Call me if an emergency comes up. But you stay out of trouble... you hear me," Grandma Eileen said, kissing Angel on the cheek before leaving.

"Don't I always so stop worrying. Love you!"

"Love you too, baby girl," her grandmother said, shutting the front door.

Angel fell back on the couch and turned on the television. Angel had gotten used to working just about every day after school for Gavin or at least hanging out with him so she wasn't sure exactly what to do with her free time. Although he gave her some money, Angel wasn't in the mood to go shopping. She thought about calling Taren, but after their altercation at school and how disgusted she was with her father, Angel squashed that idea. So she decided to eat the food her grandmother left in the oven and watch television.

Soon Angel had dozed off and fell into a deep sleep. Hours later she was awaken by the nonstop ringing of her home phone. It took Angel several minutes to finally wake up and answer the phone

"Hello," Angel answered still half asleep. She couldn't hear anybody on the other end of the phone. All she heard was a murmuring sound at first. "Hello," Angel said again.

"I've been trying to call you on your cell phone, but you weren't answering so I finally thought to call you at home."

"Taren is that you?" Angel asked, barely able to hear what she was saying.

"Yes," she sniffled.

"Are you crying? What's wrong?"

"He's dead. My father is dead!" Taren wailed, causing Angel to drop her phone in disbelief. She knew that Gavin would make Taren's father face consequences for stealing from him, but never did Angel believe death would be his punishment.

Chapter Eight

Broken Silence

"I've been waiting for you to say something, but I see that you're not so I'll start the conversation," Gavin said as he and Angel were on their way to Miami.

"We don't have to talk about it," Angel quickly said, preferring to keep things the way they were. It had been over a month since Taren's father had been murdered and although Angel was almost positive Gavin was behind it she remained silent.

"But we do. You're an important member of

my team and this has to be discussed."

"Okay, I'm listening."

"You know I'm the reason why Ronnie is dead."

"Why did you have to kill him? You knew he was my best friend's father. I can hardly even look her in the face."

"I know his death has put you in a fucked up predicament, but it had to be done. He stole from me and then he tried to break down the trust in my organization by placing the blame on you. That's a pussy nigga. I couldn't let somebody like that continue to walk these streets. He left me no choice but to end his life."

"I feel like you could've done something else besides ending his life."

"Angel, you a very smart young lady. You know the game I'm in and that you're in too," Gavin reminded her. "Part of being a boss means you have the balls to make decisions that others can't stomach. If someone steals from you, they must be dealt with. That's one of the biggest signs of disrespect in business and disrespect can never be tolerated."

"I get that, it's just..." Angel went silent.

"It's just what?"

"Taren is my best friend and she's going through a really difficult time. She adored her father. The fact that I know what happened to him..." Angel shook her head without finishing her thought.

"Who are you loyal to?" Gavin questioned.

"I'm loyal to you... always."

"Then that's all you need to be concerned about. You can be there for your friend. I'm sure she needs all the emotional support she can get right now. But what happened to her father remains between our family. What happens in this family, stays in this family. There is no broken silence."

For the duration of the drive to Miami, Angel didn't say a word. Her loyalty was to Gavin and she would never reveal what she knew, but that didn't ease her guilt regarding Taren. Her father was living a lie, but maybe it was better that his death remained a lie too or at least that's what Angel told herself.

"Taren, what's going on over here?" Angel asked when she entered the townhouse and saw a couple men packing things up in boxes. "I saw a U-Haul truck out front. Are you going somewhere?"

"We're moving," Taren revealed, walking upstairs. Angel followed Taren to her bedroom. "My mom can't afford to stay here now that my dad is..." Taren couldn't say the word. "Instead of getting evicted, we're moving in with my auntie until my mom can figure out what to do next," she said taking clothes out of her drawers and putting them into a box.

"I'm so sorry, Taren."

"Sorry that my dad is no longer here or that we're flat broke," she scoffed.

"Both, but I'm sure your mom has some money saved."

"Nope, she has nothing. Do you know she has to get rid of her BMW too because she can't afford the car note. She relied on my dad for everything and now that he's gone..." Taren swallowed hard as her eyes watered up. "Gosh, I hate saying that, but it's true my dad is dead and he's not coming back. My mom keeps telling me to toughen up and deal, but he was everything to me. What am I supposed to do now," Taren said staring off as if in a daze.

"It will be okay," Angel said walking over and hugging her friend tightly.

"That's the thing, I don't know if it's going to be okay. What is my mother going to do for work? How is she going to take care of us? We can't live with my auntie forever. Do you know I had to give my mother the $200 my dad had given me the last time I saw him?"

"I had no idea things were so tight over here. Why didn't you tell me?"

"That's not exactly something you want to share with the world."

"I'm not the world, I'm your best friend. You can tell me anything. Listen, I have some money saved. I can give you a thousand dollars."

"You have a fuckin' thousand dollars you can give me! Are you serious?" Taren's mouth dropped. Angel actually had a lot more than that saved up. She wanted to give it to her grandmother so they could get out of their rundown neighborhood and upgrade to a much nicer place. But until Angel could come up with a believable story to explain to her grandmother where she got all the cash, she kept stacking her paper.

"Yes, I'm serious and I want you to have it. I feel so guilty that you and your mother are struggling like this."

"Why do you feel guilty? The only person to blame is the sonofabitch that murdered my father. I swear I hope the police find the killer or killers soon so they can rot in jail for the rest of their lives."

"Do the police have any leads?"

"Not yet, but they're working on it or at least I hope they are."

"Why do you say it like that?"

"Because my mom said that the police are saying they think his murder is drug related. But my father was a businessman, he didn't sell drugs. I just hope they don't sweep his case to the side because they think he's some street thug."

"I know it's easier said than done, but try not to stress yourself over it. Everything will work out the way it's supposed to."

"If that's true then whoever took my father away from me will end up dead or in jail."

"I'ma go home and get that money for you. If I don't bring it back today then I'll definitely be back tomorrow."

"I really do appreciate that, Angel. My mother is going to be so happy. You really are the best, best friend."

"Thanks." Angel smiled.

"Maybe you can do something else for me too," Taren said.

"Sure, anything. What is it?"

"I know I use to talk a lot of shit when it came to your boss Gavin, but do you think maybe you can get me a job with him?"

"You know business has kinda slowed down.

I don't think he's hiring anymore people right now."

"But maybe you can put a good word in for me. Angel, we really need the money. I mean the thousand dollars you're giving us is beyond great, but you can't keep giving me that type of money. And we both know my mother has limited job skills. I can't ever remember her working."

"I'll see what I can do," Angel said reluctantly.

"You will! Thank you so much!" Taren said running over and giving Angel a big hug. "I know you can't promise anything, but I just appreciate you trying."

"No problem. I better get going. I want to get that money in your hands sooner rather than later. Talk to you soon," Angel said hurrying out because she felt the walls were closing in on her.

Chapter Nine

Got Yo' Back

"So what do you think of the new place?" Gavin asked Angel as they sat outside under the covered patio, looking at the large pool that had a solar heater.

"It's beautiful, but you already know that."

"It's not that ridiculous estate the Arcia brothers have, but I think it's a step in the right direction," Gavin said with a half smile.

"I think it's more than a step in the right direction." Angel smiled back, loving the new home Gavin had gotten in a private gated community in Davie, Florida. It was a suburb about 20 minutes outside of Sunrise. It had a chef's dream kitchen, which Gavin was adamant about having since he loved to cook. There was a media room, gym, entertaining area with design finishes throughout. Built-in niches, marble floors and four garages to fit all of Gavin's cars since he was on his way to being a collector.

"I'm glad you approve. Hopefully you'll come and keep me company often."

"You have more than enough room. It's what? Five or six bedrooms? You have all this space with no kids. It might be time for you to settle down and start a family."

"I'm too young to settle down. But if and when I meet the right woman, at least I already have a home we can call our own. Until then it's just me, and my lil' sis."

"You're so silly. Well as long as you come pick me up, I'll visit as much as you like, especially if you're going to be cooking some of those Dominican dishes I love so much."

"You saw my kitchen. I'ma be cooking everything up in there."

"I know you are and I'm here for it. But I'm really happy for you. It's nice to see what all your hustling and grinding has gotten you. You doing big things my brotha. I can't wait until I can get me and grandmother out the hood."

"Man, I done told you a million times to just say the word and I'll get you a new crib."

"I know, but like I told you, I have to be careful with my grandmother. She won't move anywhere if she thinks I got the money doing some shady shit. I'll figure it out though. But in the meantime you might be able to help me out with something else."

"What's up?"

"Well, Taren and her mom have fallen on really tough times without her dad around. Her mother wasn't working and she couldn't afford where they was living so they had to move."

"See, that's the type of bullshit I'm talkin' 'bout. That's why I'm always stressin' to you to make yo' own fuckin' money. You don't never know what's gon' happen to a nigga. This man die and leave his kid out here wit' nothin'." Gavin frowned.

"I already gave them a little money to help out, but it won't last that long."

"So what you want me to make a contribution to their pity fund. I guess I can do that." Gavin shrugged.

"I know when Malinda first introduced us she said we were friends. That wasn't exactly true."

"I already knew that. You and Malinda didn't really seem like you all had the type of personalities that would click."

"So why did you let me work for you if you knew we weren't being straight up?"

"'Cause I knew you would be a good fit for me and that's all I gave a fuck about. And look, I was right."

"Well, Taren was the one who told me about the job because Malinda had come to her, but she declined because at the time she didn't need the money, but I did."

"Now that her situation has changed, shorty want the job... right?"

"Something like that."

"So let me get this straight. You want me to give a job to the daughter of the man I had killed," Gavin said putting his beer down on the table.

"No, not really. I think it's a bad idea, but I also know that Taren and her mom are in a really fucked up situation. I feel bad for them and Taren came through for me by hooking me up with this job so I think I should at least try and do the same for her."

"You don't seem to be trying that hard," Gavin huffed.

"Like I said, I don't think it's a good idea."

"Why, you don't think your friend is reliable

to do her job?"

"No, it's not that. I think Taren would do what she's supposed to do."

"Then why don't you think it's a good idea?" Gavin pressed for an answer.

"Because like you pointed out, she's the daughter of the man you had killed. I think that would be a little uncomfortable."

"Uncomfortable for who... not for me. It ain't like she know I had her father killed. So I guess you mean, it will be uncomfortable for you."

"Maybe so."

"Do you wanna help your friend enough to get over being uncomfortable?"

"Of course I want to help Taren. I hate seeing her in this fucked up predicament, but I don't have a good feeling about it. It's your call though."

Gavin sat quiet for a few minutes as if in deep thought. He took a few more gulps of beer and then stood up. "Tell her she has the job."

"Are you sure?"

"I wouldn't have said what I said if I wasn't. Now you just make sure you can keep it together."

"Gavin, I know how to handle my business. If you want Taren to work for you, say no more, I'll deal with it."

"I knew you were my soldier." Gavin winked. "Now come ride wit' me to pick this money up.

Then we can stop and get something to eat."

"I take it you're not cooking tonight. Well I don't know if I can ride with you then. You can just drop me off at home." Angel laughed.

"Oh word... how 'bout we eat at that spot you like so much."

"Now you talking. Let's go!" Angel said, grabbing Gavin's arm.

"Stay right here. I won't be gone, but for a second," Gavin said getting out the car.

"Cool," Angel said, turning up the Jeezy CD, bopping her head rapping along to the lyrics. Between listening to the music and responding to text messages, Angel was oblivious to how much time had passed. It wasn't until she heard what sounded like gunshots that her attention was directed towards the apartment Gavin had gone inside of.

Angel's eyes darted all around trying to see where the popping noise came from. Then she heard what sounded like a loud thump and a man came tumbling out the front door and he appeared to be hurt, but Angel couldn't see his face. Her heart started racing because she wasn't sure if it was Gavin who was hurt or if he was doing the hurting. Not wanting to take any chances Angel grabbed the gun that Gavin kept in the secret compartment of his car.

Angel tiptoed towards the apartment, trying to remain inconspicuous as she sneaked on the scene. As she got closer she saw a man come out holding a gun and pointing it down at the man on the ground.

"Fuck you man! You bitch nigga!"

"Yeah I'm the same bitch nigga that got yo' money, drugs and 'bout to take yo' life," the man shouted, but before he could pull the trigger, Angel jumped out the darkness and started blasting. Once she began releasing the hot lead it was like her finger had a mind of its own. Angel couldn't stop firing until she emptied the chamber on her target.

"Gavin, are you okay!" Angel screamed, kneeling down next to him. She could see blood all over his shirt and on his jeans.

"He got me in the chest and the leg, but I'll be okay. Just help me to the car. I'll tell you where to drive." Luckily for them, although Angel wasn't 16 and didn't have her driver's license, Gavin had already taught her how to drive so she was able to get them to their destination.

"You're losing a lot of blood. Are you sure I shouldn't take you to the emergency room?"

Angel was trying to keep her composure and not freak out, but seeing all the blood gushing out made it difficult.

"No! Just drive. The place you taking me, they'll be able to fix me up. The last thing we need is to be getting interrogated by the police."

"Okay," Angel said knowing Gavin was right. Not only were drugs involved, but she also killed a man. Angel was now a murderer and there was no turning back from her living a life of crime.

Chapter Ten

Saddest Day

2 Years Later...

"Girl, I can't believe we'll be graduating in a couple months. Senior year flew by," Taren said, as the girls sat in the chair at the nail salon getting pedicures.

"You ain't lying. I can't believe this time next year I'll be in college."

"So have you decided where you're going?"

"Yep, University Of Miami on a full scholarship."

"Who would ever guess your hustling ass would get a full scholarship to school. Goes to show never judge a book by its cover."

"Hard work does pay off although I wish I could get my grandmother from working so hard. It's like the more I try to help her out with the bills the harder she works."

"Hell, all the money you make she don't even have to work," Taren sniped.

"True, but she can't know that."

"It's crazy that you've been doing your dirt for over three years and you've managed to keep it under the radar from her."

"Yeah, but that's because instead of indulging in over the top material things I stack my paper. I keep it cute, but not so extravagant it would raise red flags. 'Cause you know my grandmother nosey as hell."

"I don't know how you do it. I'm not pulling nearly as much as you, but the money I do make runs through my fingers like water."

"Taren, you don't have to tell me. Every time I see you, you got a new designer bag or some new shoes. You have to work just to bankroll your shopping addiction."

"Why you sound surprised? I've been like

this since we were little kids. Remember my father used to take me shopping like every week," Taren said as her face lit up.

"I remember. He definitely spoiled you rotten."

"Sure did. Sometimes I still forget he's gone. I might see something I want and I'll reach for my phone to call and ask him to get it for me. Then I remember if I call he wouldn't pick up," Taren said somberly. "Enough of this sad talk, we supposed to be getting all dolled up for this party Gavin's taking us to tonight. I'm excited."

"It should be nice. He said it's at that new upscale nightclub everybody been talking about."

"I heard all the cute dudes with paper be going there and hopefully I'll be going home with one tonight," Taren said grinding her hips.

"There you go on yo' hoe shit. Are you going to ever settle down and get one boyfriend?" Angel questioned.

"Sure am, when I can find one man that can cover my shopping expenses, living expenses and blow my mind in bed. Until then, I'll be a single girl dating multiple men," Taren winked.

"You're a mess, Taren, but then again you already know that."

"So are you picking me up or are we meeting at Gavin's house."

"I have some business I need to handle for Gavin so we can meet at his house. Then we can leave from there and all go to the party together."

"Sounds like a plan. Now let's sit back and enjoy our pedicures because we have a busy night ahead of us."

After hanging out with Taren for most of the day it was back to business for Angel. She pulled up to the parking lot at the strip mall to meet a customer for Gavin. Angel was hoping they would arrive soon because she still needed to make a couple more stops before getting ready for the party. She eyed the clock on the car dashboard and saw the guy was 20 minutes late. She was about to place a call when she saw Gavin pulling up next to her.

"What are you doing here?" Angel questioned, stepping out her car. "What, you didn't trust me to handle your business." She smiled.

"You know I trust you about as much as I trust myself," he shot back, leaning against the car.

"Well you can keep me company while I wait

for this customer to show up."

"He's not coming," Gavin said casually.

"What? Man he got me out here wasting my time. I got so much shit to do. Ain't nobody got time for that," Angel smacked.

"It's not a complete waste of your time. You were never supposed to meet a customer. I just told you that to get you here for my surprise. It didn't work out how I planned. But hey, shit happens."

"Gavin, what in the world are you rambling on about?"

"Man, listen. You know I ain't the sentimental type, but you about to be graduating soon, going to college wit' a full scholarship. You managed to do all that while being my right hand girl. When I first met you, you were a kid with so much potential and now you're a young lady about to enter womanhood. I love you like my lil' sister, but I'm feeling like a proud papa."

"That means a lot to me. I have to give you credit though. You always gave me the best advice which kept me motivated to do better and keep my eye on the prize."

"And you have so you should be rewarded."

"Trust me when I look at all the money I have saved, you have rewarded me tremendously."

"You earned every dollar of that money. But

this right here is my gift to you," Gavin stated, dangling a car key.

"Hold up," Angel said glancing at the spanking new red convertible BMW. "You got this for me! You are the best!" she beamed.

"Yep, it's all yours. You deserve this and so much more. I know you don't like to talk about it, but I'll never forget that night you saved my life."

"I did what I had to do. You would've done the same for me."

"This ain't about what I woulda done it's about what you did. You didn't let fear take over. I know so called hard niggas that wouldn't have had enough balls to pull the trigger, but you did. I'm telling you, you were born a fighter it's in your DNA."

"I must've gotten it from my father because my grandmother said my mother was so sweet and such a pushover, that she couldn't hurt a fly. I would give anything just to spend one day with both of them. But that's never gonna happen so there's no sense in me thinking about it. What I can think about is this sick ride you got me."

"She is a beauty, just like her new owner. You ready to take her for a ride?" Gavin asked handing Angel the key.

"Yes, I am, but what will I tell my grandmother? When she sees me pull up in this car, she's gonna have a fit."

"Tell her a friend let you borrow it. The good news is you'll be off to college in a few months so she won't know what you driving."

"I think I can hold my grandmother off until then. So I'll take this car off your hands and I guess you'll be going home in this," Angel said tossing Gavin the key to her old Nissan Sentra.

"This shit bet not break down on me."

"For over a year it's been reliable transportation for me so think positive. Now let me get out of here so I can go stunt on everybody in my new car. I'll see you and Taren later on tonight at your house," Angel said, blowing Gavin a goodbye kiss before speeding off in her car.

Angel had the top down and music blasting when she pulled into her apartment complex. After leaving Gavin she ran some errands and spent another couple hours riding around showing off. Even though she wasn't going to tell her grandmother the BMW was hers, she couldn't wait to let her see it and take her for a ride. As Angel was putting the top up she noticed a police car pulling up next to her. She continued about her business until she saw they were headed in the same direction as her.

"Can I help you with something?" Angel asked standing in front of her apartment door.

"Is this where Eileen Riviera lives?"

"Yes, she's my grandmother."

"Your grandmother was involved in an accident. On her way to work today she had a heart attack."

"Oh goodness! Is she okay? What hospital is she at? I have to go see her," Angel said panicking.

"We're sorry, she didn't make it."

"Are you saying my grandmother is dead... no this is some sort of mistake. My grandmother can't be dead," Angel kept saying over and over again. "Please just go! This isn't happening," Angel screamed, struggling to get the key in the lock to open the door.

The police officers watched Angel for a few minutes making sure she wasn't going to have a breakdown and need some medical assistance. After they felt she was in the clear they got in their car and drove off, but Angel was barely holding it together. She felt like she wanted to vomit, but nothing would come up. Angel fell to the floor and laid in the fetal position as the tears wouldn't stop falling. Angel reached for her cell phone to call the only person she knew could help her get through this pain.

"Answer the phone, Gavin," she cried, needing to hear his voice. After calling him a few more times and not getting an answer, Angel got herself together and drove to his house. When she got there she saw Taren's car out front and remembered they were supposed to be going to a party tonight, she had forgotten that quickly.

I guess it worked out that both of my best friends are here to help me get through this, Angel thought to herself using the key Gavin had given her to get in. There were a bunch of lights on in the house and there was music playing, but there was no sign of Gavin or Taren.

Angel walked back to the kitchen then outside by the pool until going upstairs. Gavin's bedroom door was cracked open and when Angel stepped inside, it was as if she had walked into a nightmare.

"Angel, I had to do it," Taren wailed, standing over Gavin with a gun.

"Taren, what have you done!" Angel screamed, running over to them. "Oh gosh, he's dead. You killed Gavin!" Angel cried out.

"I had to. He's responsible for my father's murder. He admitted it to me. I had to kill him," Taren wept.

"Taren, what have you done. What have you

done," Angel continued saying between tears as she held Gavin's dead body in her arms.

Chapter Eleven

The Art Of Letting Go

Angel sat on the bench at the park staring out at the lake. It was the first moment of peace she had in what seemed like forever. The sky was clear, you could hear the birds chirping and you could feel a cool breeze that seemed to soothe the soul. Angel needed this time to think and figure out how she would be able to move forward with so much loss behind her. She had to say goodbye to the two most important people in her life, her grandmother and Gavin and now she would have to say goodbye to her best friend.

"I was surprised you wanted to meet here," Taren said unintentionally interrupting Angel's thoughts.

"Sit down," Angel said, moving over to make room on the bench for Taren. "It's so peaceful here, I thought it would be the perfect place for us to talk."

"Before you say anything, I want to thank you for not turning me in. I know how much you loved Gavin."

"I do love him... I mean I did, but I love you too. That's why this is so difficult."

"It's difficult for me too. I cared about Gavin, but when I found that watch in his drawer, my father's watch that he was wearing the night he was murdered," Taren paused trying to subdue the anger that was about to boil up again. "Then Gavin had the nerve to say that he got what he deserved because my father was a thief and a liar. How dare he. My father was a good man."

"And so was Gavin. He was my family. He was the closest thing that I ever had to a father in my life. I knew this was never going to work, but I had to look out for you and now Gavin is dead," Angel said angrily.

"Why did you know it wasn't going to work?"

"Because Gavin wasn't lying. Your father was

a drug dealer. That's how he made his money. Not from running a successful car dealership or any other business. He was buying drugs from Gavin. Then he stole money and blamed me for it. That's who your father really was."

"Why are you saying these things?" Taren barked.

"Because it's the truth. Did I think Gavin should've had your father killed... no. But that wasn't my decision to make. He didn't steal from me he stole from him, but he did lie on me. If Gavin had believed your father over me, it might've been my funeral you would've been attending."

"So you knew Gavin was going to kill my father?"

"No! I only found out when you called and told me. I was shocked."

"When you found out Gavin was responsible why didn't you tell me?"

"Because my loyalty was to Gavin. He made a business decision and I respected that. What your father did was wrong, and in the business we're in that can never be tolerated. He was well aware how this game worked so much so that he was willing to throw me to the wolves in order to steal from his connect."

"I don't believe that," Taren said shaking her head in denial.

"I have no reason to lie to you. I was the one doing the pick up and drop offs with your father. He asked me not to tell you what his true profession was and I honored that. He honored nothing."

"This is too much. None of this makes sense," Taren cried.

"It makes perfect sense to me. My only regret is that I went to Gavin to get you the job. If I hadn't he would still be alive. I had a bad feeling about it, but never did I think it would end with Gavin dead and you being responsible for his murder."

"Well I regret ever working for the man who took my father away from me," Taren yelled.

"You don't get it, but how could you. You're so selfish and self-centered," Angel said in frustration, turning her head.

"Excuse me! Are you blaming me for this?"

"No, I blame myself. But none of that matters now. Gavin's gone, my grandmother's gone, there's nothing left here for me."

"What about me? We're still best friends... aren't we?" Taren questioned.

"I know how much you loved your father and for that reason I forgive you for killing Gavin. But I can't be around you right now. It's time for me to move on."

"Move on without me in your life?"

"Yes, at least for now. Maybe with time my feelings will change, but right now I'm so angry with you. I'm sorry," Angel said and walked away.

Angel looked around the empty apartment she shared with her grandmother all her life one last time before hitting the road. All of her bags were packed and in the car and Angel was ready to go. She would've left town the same day both her grandmother and Gavin died, but she knew her grandmother would want her to finish high school so she stayed until graduation. At first Angel no longer had a desire to utilize her full scholarship for college, but she remembered how proud her grandmother was and the way her face lit up when she told her the news. For that reason alone, Angel decided to follow through with college plans.

On her drive to Miami, Angel contemplated her next move. School was a given, but that ambitious spirit in her needed more. Because she didn't feel any financial pressure, Angel let her mind roam free about what her next hustle would be. She considered starting a business, but wasn't sure exactly what she would want it to be.

After Angel had saved his life, Gavin told her where he kept a large sum of money and if anything happened to him, he wanted her to have it. That money combined with all the money Angel had saved while she worked for Gavin gave her some very heavy pockets. So heavy that she had more than enough to invest in any business venture she decided to start. But even at her young age, Angel was savvy when it came to making money. She didn't want to invest in anything that wasn't going to bring in a profit. So she sat back in her convertible BMW letting the wind blow through her hair, determined to figure out what her next come up would be.

Chapter Twelve

New Bitch

Angel arrived in Miami feeling like a new bitch. Although the city was so close to Sunrise where she grew up it felt like she was a thousand miles away. The few times she did come to the city, she was always with Gavin and they were in and out handling business. Angel never had the opportunity to take in the city, the people and all that it had to offer. Now that she did, it seemed like one big endless playground of fun.

Angel settled nicely in her one-bedroom loft

in a luxury building on Bay Rd. It had a balcony with an ocean view and all. Since she didn't have a job, she had to go through the sublease route. The guy was initially hesitant to let Angel move in. But when she pulled out the cash and was willing to pay up front for the first year, he couldn't hand those keys over fast enough. She spent most of the summer decorating her new place, indulging in her urge to buy designer clothes—being that she suppressed it before because she didn't want her grandmother to find out what she was doing—and lounging by the pool which had become her favorite thing to do.

"Is anyone sitting here?" a girl asked Angel, pointing to the chaise lounge next to her.

"Nope, it's all yours. Although there are a few other empty chairs over there," Angel commented not understanding why the girl wanted this particular chair.

"Yeah, I know, but this chair is getting direct sunlight and I really wanted to work on my tan," the girl explained.

Angel slightly moved down her sunglasses to get a good look at who she was talking to. She was a cute, petite white girl, with breasts that were clearly too large for her tiny frame.

"By all means get your tan on," Angel said sliding her sunglasses back over her eyes as she continued reading her fashion magazine.

"I'm Laurie, what's your name?" the girl asked after getting comfortable in the chair.

"Angel," she said sharply.

"So Angel, do you live here or are you just visiting someone in the building, like me?" Laurie giggled, not taking the hint that Angel didn't want to be bothered.

"I live here."

"Really?! Wow, what do you do for a living? This place is pricey."

"I'm in school."

"What you have rich parents or a rich boyfriend?"

"I don't mean to be rude, but I'm really into this magazine."

"Oh... so you wanna be left alone?"

"Yes, pretty much... thanks."

"I won't bother you. I'm going to lay here and work on my tan," Laurie said sounding extra bubbly. Angel ignored her and kept flipping through her magazine. "Hate to be a pain but would you please do me a big favor?" Laurie asked in an almost begging tone.

"What is it?" Angel questioned rolling her eyes.

"Can you put this suntan lotion on my back?" Angel sat up and the girl was lying on her stomach topless. She wasn't in the mood to do anything for this chick, but Angel figured the quicker she complied, the quicker she would leave her alone."

"Sure, give me the lotion," Angel said, tossing her magazine down.

"So what are you studying in school?" Laurie asked making small talk.

"It's my first year so I haven't decided my major yet."

"I wish I would've went to school, but academics were never my thing. I'm more of a party girl, you know."

"I guess. I've never been much into parties."

"Really and you decided to go to school in Miami. This city is party central. You know what, you should come out with us tonight," Laurie turned around and said, damn near popping Angel in the face with her breasts.

"That's sweet, but I think I'ma just stay in tonight."

"No, please come. I know you don't know me, but you seem really cool. I'm going to be the only girl tonight so having you there would be great. You would be doing me a huge favor and I would like totally appreciate it."

"You don't have any other girlfriends?"

"Normally my roommate Aspen would come with me, but she had a date tonight and I only moved here a year ago so I don't really have any other friends."

"I'm sorry, what did you say your name was again?"

"Laurie," she beamed.

"Laurie, you seem sweet, but honestly I'm not the party type. I wouldn't be any fun. Trust me, you'll be better off going without me."

"I tell you what. Just come with me to the club and if you don't like it, you can stay ten minutes and leave. Pleasssssse," she pleaded.

"Fine." Angel couldn't believe she agreed to go with some chick she just met by the pool. But there was something endearing about the girl. Maybe it was her bubbly personality or her sweet nature, but Angel found herself wanting to do her a favor.

"Awww you're the best!" Laurie beamed giving Angel a hug.

"No problem," Angel said moving back as she was not comfortable having Laurie's exposed breasts pressed against her chest.

"We're leaving at 11. You can either come to the guy's apartment I'm staying at or you can meet us in the lobby."

"I'll meet you guys in the lobby."

"Okay, but Angel, please don't stand me up," she said getting a sad puppy dog look on her face.

"I'm not going to stand you up, Laurie. I'll be there."

"Awesome! We're going to have a great time tonight. You'll see," Laurie said cheerfully.

When the small entourage arrived at King Of Diamonds on NE 5th Avenue, Angel was feeling some type of way. She had no idea that when Laurie said they were going to a club she meant strip club. Angel had nothing against strippers, but her idea of fun wasn't watching a bunch of naked women gyrate on stage although she had to admit, some of their pole skills were extremely impressive.

Once the group was seated, bottle service got popping, and Angel had a couple glasses of champagne in her system, her mood began to soften. It was Make It Rain Thursday at the club and that's what damn near every man in there was doing, including the four NFL players Angel and Laurie came with. They were seated in a long blue couch in front of the pole so the men had easy access to all the ass they wanted.

"Are you having a good time?" Laurie

screamed, wanting to be heard over the loud music and boisterous crowd.

"Yes!" Angel nodded and she was telling the truth. She had never been exposed to anything like this before. Watching women put on a performance in damn near seven-inch high heels and men throwing money at them nonstop for it was an eye opener for Angel. For the duration of the night, she spent half her time observing her surroundings and how the dancers and customers interacted and the rest of the time partying with Laurie.

Now she understood why Laurie was so desperate to have her tag along. Even though they came with some guys, all their attention was on the tits and ass sashaying across the floor. Laurie knew she couldn't compete with that so she wanted to have someone keep her company and Angel couldn't blame her.

They partied at KOD for about three hours before stopping at a late night diner for breakfast food and then heading back to the crib. At first Angel was going to go to her own apartment, but Laurie convinced her to hang out a bit longer so she went to the top floor with them where one of the NFL players lived.

"Wow, this place is massive," Angel commented when they got to his penthouse apartment.

"Yeah, I love and I hate visiting his place because when go back home I get reminded how broke I am," Laurie said, taking a seat.

"You're funny."

"I'm serious, but at least I get to have a good time. Are you glad you listened and came out with us?"

"I am. Surprisingly I had a really good time."

"Does that mean we can hang out again?" Laurie asked.

"Definitely."

"How about—" Before Laurie could finish her sentence, the NFL player who lived at the apartment yelled out her name.

"Laurie, come here."

"Let me go see what he wants," Laurie said, heading back to his bedroom.

"So Angel, how long have you known Laurie," one of the other players asked Angel once she was alone.

"Not long, but she's a cool chick."

"Yeah, you seem cool yourself."

"Thanks. You're Dawson right?" Angel asked wanting to make sure she wasn't confusing the names.

"That's me. I'm the one you danced with at the club. You don't remember that."

"Yeah, I remember. I was just confirming

your name. I did meet four of you at the same time."

"I know, I'm just playing with you."

"So Laurie said you live in the building too."

"I stay on the 11th floor."

"That's what's up. You like living here?"

"I do, it's really nice."

"Yeah, it is. I gotta spot in here too. I'm one floor down."

"What? They had some sort of special going on? How ya'll end up in the same building?" Angel wanted to know.

"Nah, won't no special going on," Dawson laughed. "Our man Andre got a place first. When we came to visit we was like damn we want a place up in this joint too, so that's what we did."

"I feel you."

"Since you our neighbor you gotta come visit us sometimes. We cool people to hang out with."

"For sure. I recently moved to Miami so I don't know anybody. At least now I know I can come visit my neighbors."

"Exactly, here take my number," Dawson said giving Angel his digits.

They spent the next hour discussing everything from sports, women, food, and even movies. They had a good vibe. Nothing sexual they just clicked on a friendship level.

More and more Angel was feeling like she made the right decision moving to Miami. She was discovering new shit and new people. Angel welcomed the change and was looking forward to uncovering what else she had been missing.

Chapter Thirteen

Run Yo' Shit

"Thanks for meeting me for brunch," Laurie said when Angel got to the table. She had asked Angel to meet her at Tongue & Cheek on Washington Ave. It was her favorite brunch spot because not only was the food delicious, for $20 you get unlimited Bloody Mary's, Mimosas and Bellini's, which meant everything to a social alcoholic like Laurie.

"No problem, I was hungry anyway," Angel said going through the menu.

"Of course, get what you like, but the chicken and cheddar waffles, crab benedict, and the sticky-icky bun with brown butter pecan are all super tasty," Laurie said, already on her second Mimosa.

"Thanks for the recommendations. I think I'll keep it simple and have some buttermilk pancakes she said putting down the menu.

"I want to apologize again for taking so long to come back out. When Dawson told me you went home I felt horrible."

"Laurie, I told you it's no big deal. It was nothing, but an elevator ride down. Dawson kept me company anyway. He's cool."

"Dawson is cool. He liked you a lot. He's a lot nicer than Ace."

"Ace is the one you're dating, right?"

"I wouldn't call it dating, we hang out sometimes."

"Not to get all in your business, but I'm assuming you were gone so long because you guys were having sex?" Angel asked.

"Yeah, was I loud? Could you hear us?"

"No, we couldn't hear anything. So did you get anything before you left Ace's apartment?"

"Get anything... anything like what?" Laurie looked puzzled.

"You know like money."

"Are you kidding... is that a joke?"

"No, I'm serious. "

"Why would Ace pay me to have sex? He is a known NFL player he can have sex with anyone he wants."

"He should pay you for the same reason him and his friends were throwing all that money at those strippers. You put in just as much work as they did. So why did they get paid and you didn't?" Angel questioned.

Laurie sat dumbfounded for a minute trying to analyze what Angel said. It never dawned on her to make the comparison, but if it wasn't about dollars it made no sense to Angel.

"Listen, you know nothing serious is going to come out of your relationship with Ace so why not get something out the deal. You love sex, but yet you're always screaming broke. I just think you can do better, Laurie. Make your enjoyment of sex and partying work for you instead of against you."

"How are those things working against me?"

"If you're fucking rich guys for fun yet you're always broke then you're hustling backwards."

"But rich, famous guys don't have to pay for sex."

"Ummm did you not see all that money they were tossing out at King Of Diamonds?

What do you think those women are selling? It ain't fuckin' girl scout cookies. Understand something, rich men don't pay for pussy because they have to they pay for it so they don't have to be inconvenienced. It's easier to hire someone to do a sexual service because once both sides have honored their part of the arrangement, the man can get rid of the woman without the headache of feeling obligated to be nice. It's a win, win situation for both parties involved."

"You make it sound like a business."

"It is, it's called prostitution and it's still one of the most profitable businesses around."

"I'm not a prostitute," Laurie declared.

"Well you should be. I respect a woman more who puts a value to what's between her legs than someone who is constantly having casual sex, but yet has nothing to show for it. It's one thing if you're having sex with your boyfriend, then these rules wouldn't apply, but as you stated Ace is not your man. He's just some rich guy you're having casual sex with."

"Maybe you have a point, but there is no way Ace is going to start paying me now after he's been getting it for free all this time."

"True but fuck Ace. There are hundreds of other Aces out there," Angel said, as the wheels started turning in her head. On her ride to Miami she kept trying to figure out a business she could start and invest her money in, but would guarantee a profit. Angel thought she finally figured out what her next come up would be.

"There are a lot of escort services in Miami, but I don't want to have sex with a bunch of old boring rich men."

"I feel you on that and you wouldn't have to if I have anything to do with it."

"Are you saying you're going to start an escort service?" Laurie asked becoming intrigued.

"Why not? I just have to build a clientele. But all it takes is one guy to tell another guy and pretty soon word of mouth will have business flourishing. I can make it some exclusive shit where I only cater to athletes, entertainers, and industry execs. I get the baddest chicks in Miami, who like you, don't want to have sex with boring old men for money. They want to deal exclusively with elite men that they would normally fuck for free. But I'll broker the deals so we can all get paid," Angel said with certainty.

"You really think you can pull this off?"

"I sure can and I know exactly who is going to help me. But before that I have to get my girls. Once I have the women, the men will come."

"Well you already have one because I'm so down. It sounds too good to be true, but I hope you can make it happen. I know my roommate Aspen would want to join because she's always scheming to get money out of men."

"I know a couple of girls at my school that would definitely jump at the opportunity. Once I get a few girls on lock they'll start spreading the word and more and more girls will be coming. Pretty soon these chicks will be trying to pay me to join. I'm going to run this shit," Angel said without hesitation.

"To be so young, you sure are about your business. Making that work would be genius."

"I will make it work. I'm going to call my escort service, Angel's Girls. I'll get some cute business cards made and a website. Only top of the line chicks will represent my company. I'll be the spot that all the so-called cool people will want to get their girls from. I'll have Angel's Girls open for business in no time.

Chapter Fourteen

Angel's Girls

"First of all, congratulations ladies for being a part of Angel's Girls. Look around because you all should be proud of yourselves. Hundreds of women applied for a position, but only some qualified and the chosen few are sitting right here. I picked a variation of beauties that represent the rainbow and each of you is special in your own way.

"Each of you have been given a pamphlet that gives you an overview about the company, but most importantly it states the rules that each of you much follow if you want to maintain a position within the organization. I will be enforcing the three strikes you're out so I suggest if you're interested in holding on to your job, read the information carefully," Angel strongly suggested. "Does anyone have any questions?" A woman quickly raised her hand. "Yes, Trista?"

"When will we start work?" she wanted to know and so did the other girls based on their reaction to her question.

"You all will go through a training course which will entail an intense etiquette class for two weeks. Mrs. Sinclair will be overseeing the class and she will grade each of you when it's over. At the end of the course if Mrs. Sinclair believes you're not a good fit for the class then you will be dismissed. You will also be paid a fee for each day you attend class. Everyone will also receive an initial budget for wardrobe and other personal products you may need. All clothes must be approved prior to purchase. Are we clear?" Angel questioned, making eye contact with each girl one by one.

"I'm just ready to work, so whatever you say," Autumn said voicing the feelings of the rest of the women in the room.

"Then let's get you ladies at the top of your

game." Angel smiled, proud of the group of women she had handpicked for her new business venture. She was amazed at how fast things came together and how everything was coming along so smoothly. She had to credit Dawson for the majority of her success in regards to immediately obtaining clients. With him being an NFL player he had friends on several of the teams, but not only football players but NBA, soccer, baseball, and even hockey. Dawson was also cool with a bunch of rappers so he put Angel on to them too. The men were simply waiting for the green light that Angel's Girls was open for business and Angel planned on making that happen soon enough, but she wanted things to be done right.

Angel envisioned running a sophisticated, high-class service that made customers feel that she had the best so they were willing to pay the best. That's why it was important to her that her girls had their shit together. Keeping themselves groomed from head to toe was mandatory. Each girl had to keep their body tight, hair done, kitty groomed, clothes flawless, mani/pedi perfect and personal hygiene on point. Her girls would be selling the ultimate fantasy and all the men would be rushing to buy it.

Angel had butterflies in her stomach and there was nothing she could do to make them go away. Tonight was the official launch of Angel's Girls and she was throwing a lavish party to make her presence known. Angel had rented a gorgeous mansion on the beach for the occasion. It was an invite only event and each attendee had to pay one thousand dollars to come. Once word spread about the soiree, it became the must go to celebration. Angel knew with the competitive, ego driven men she had invited that would be exactly what would happen. The men that didn't get the initial invite felt slighted and that they were somehow not seen as important enough to come so they were willing to spend ridiculous amounts of money just so they could be a part of the so-called cool crowd.

Angel even created the ultimate VIP experience that cost $5,000. It was limited to only five men since that package included their own bedroom, five bottles of champagne and three women that were there to pleasure them for the night. Angel had everything set up to stroke the most arrogant man's ego for the night.

"Tonight is finally here ladies and I hope you're ready," Angel said speaking to her girls an hour before the party was to begin. "I must say you all look amazing," she beamed, admiring the high-end cocktail dress, and jumpsuits they were wearing. Their outfits were revealing and extremely sexy, but not trashy, which was the look Angel was going for. She had even hired a makeup and hair team to have each girl looking like a movie star for the big night. Angel was pleased with the final results.

"We're ready!" all the ladies cheered and clapped their hands anticipating the big night.

"Then let's do this!" Angel cheered back.

Angel had rented a fleet of Rolls Royces to have the girls arrive in. She wanted the women stepping out in style and that's what she made happen. When they pulled up in front of the mansion, the girls looked like they were the main chicks of a rap superstars music video, the only thing missing was the bumping music blasting.

When they entered, the event planner had decorated the place to the max. She had turned the home into a fantasy dreamland. It had a black and white theme with the finest white orchids. There were well-dressed servers and even a chef on deck to whip up whatever the guest wanted.

Angel had spent a shit load of money putting this party together, but it was well worth the investment. She sat back and relished at how wonderful the evening was turning out. The girls seemed to be having a good time and the men seemed to be living out their fantasy. The party gave Angel the perfect opportunity to let clients see firsthand what her business offered.

"I was crazy to ever doubt you. Not only did you pull this off, but I've never seen anything like it," Laurie said when she came up to Angel extra excited. "I knew I got a great feeling about you when we met at the pool. You really are that chick." Laurie winked before hurrying off to work the party.

As Angel stood in the background watching everything she couldn't help but think about Gavin and how proud of her he would be. He had always instilled in her the importance of grinding and putting your all into whatever you did so you could be the best at it. Gavin never believed in half-assing anything and Angel never forgot that. She would've given anything for him to be here to see that she was able to take her vision and execute with perfect precision.

Chapter Fifteen

Just Like Old Times

Angel was in such a deep sleep that it took her home phone ringing nonstop to finally halfway wake her up. "Hello," she answered still not fully alert.

"Ms. Riviera, there is a Taren Owens here to see you," the man who worked in the lobby informed her. It took a second for the name to resonate with Angel but once it did she woke the fuck up.

"Send her up," Angel mumbled surprised

that her old friend from Sunrise was about to be at her front door. Angel didn't even have time to get herself together before she heard the knock at the door.

"Angel, I'm so happy to see you!" Taren beamed, giving Angel a hug when she opened the door.

"How did you find me?" Angel asked hugging Taren back.

"It wasn't easy that's for sure. But I knew you were in Miami and with Google you can pretty much find anybody," Taren said.

"Well come in," Angel said taking Taren's hand. "Can I get you something to drink or to eat? Although I don't have much in the fridge."

"Some juice would be good," Taren said looking around Angel's loft. "Your apartment is so hot and that view is killer. "You seem to be doing well for yourself, Angel. I'm happy for you."

"Thanks," Angel said handing Taren a glass of orange juice. "So how are things with you?"

"Things are okay."

"How's your mom?"

"She's not good. You know she never really got it together after my father died. She's been in and out of one bad relationship after another. She won't admit it, but she's developed a real bad drinking problem over the last few months that are making things worse."

"I'm sorry to hear that."

"Me too. I remember how ideal I used to think my life was but now I don't even remember that girl," Taren said sadly.

Angel looked at her friend who was still a pretty girl, but appeared to be worn and stressed. Her normally laid hair was pulled back in an unkempt bun. Her nails were chipped and eyes were lifeless and even though Taren was always on the slim side she seemed skinnier than normal.

"Why don't we go out and spend a day of getting pampered, like we used to do," Angel suggested.

"That would be so much fun, but honestly I don't have any money to do all that," Taren admitted. "I spent most of the money I had on gas to get here. I have to keep what I have left to get back home," she said as if embarrassed.

"You don't have to worry, it's my treat," Angel said waving her hand.

"Are you sure? I don't want you going out your way for me."

"I'm positive. I want to do it. Now give me a minute to go get ready and we can head out."

Angel and Taren spent the entire day getting pampered. They began their day at Spa V at Hotel Victor. The ambiance was inviting and soothing. With scattered pillows, daybeds, and subdued lighting you couldn't help but fall into relax mode. The European influences gave the place a sultry and stylish feel that made it seem like a calming refuge. The ladies indulged themselves in an invigorating body scrub, a de-stressing stone massage and a Visage pour Homme facial. They walked out the spa feeling like brand new girls. The next stop was an upscale salon where they got their hair done, a Happy Feet peppermint foot scrub with emu oil and of course a manicure.

"This day has been unbelievable," Taren said, overwhelmed by how nice Angel was being to her.

"We're not done yet." Angel giggled. "Now it's time for the really fun part. It's time to hit the mall!"

In the few short months since Angel started her escort service, business was booming. Money was flowing like water so Angel was more than happy to spend some of it on her childhood friend. Being with Taren made her realize how much she missed having a familiar face around her. She missed her grandmother and Gavin so much that Angel tried to put all memories of her past in the back of her mind. It was too painful to remember. But having Taren back in her life filled a void for Angel.

"Angel, I don't know what to say. This day has seemed like a dream to me. I remember when my father used to do things like this for me, never did I imagine my best friend would."

"I'm glad I could put a smile on your face, because having you here put one on mine too."

"I'm so happy to hear that. I wasn't sure how you would feel when I showed up. I know when you left you pretty much hated me."

"I didn't hate you, Taren. I was angry not only with you but myself. We can't change the past and I don't want to dwell on that anger anymore. I want to let it go. I have my best friend back and that means everything to me."

"Me too," Taren said as the two girls hugged each other tightly. "I better hit the road, but I hope I can come back and visit soon."

"Do you have to leave?"

"I know you have school and whatever else you have going on. I don't want to intrude."

"Why don't you stay? Having you here has been the most fun I had in a long time."

"You're in Miami. I'm sure you've had some fun times." Taren laughed.

"Yes, of course I have, but it feels different when you're doing fun things with someone that you've known almost your entire life. I would love to have you here. We can be roommates. I know I only have one bedroom, but we can make it work."

"To live in a place like this, I'll sleep on the fuckin' floor," Taren said. "I just can't believe you want me to stay."

"I do. So will you? Will you live in Miami with me?"

"Hell yeah! There is nothing for me back in Sunrise. It's not like my mom would even notice I'm gone. I would love to start over here with you."

"Awesome! Welcome home roomie!!"

Chapter Sixteen

This Is A Warning

"Cheers ladies!" Angel said holding up her champagne glass. "It's our six month anniversary and business is better than ever," she said to a few of the girls she took out for dinner. "You all are my most requested and biggest moneymakers and I wanted to show you my appreciation. Please take these," Angel said handing envelopes to the seven ladies sitting around the table.

"Two thousand dollars!" Alicia yelled when she opened the envelope and counted the cash.

"You gave each of us two thousand dollars?" Laurie gushed, glancing over at Aspen.

"Yes, it's a bonus to let you know your hard work hasn't gone unnoticed," Angel stated.

"You're the absolute best boss," Aspen declared. "I can't imagine working for anyone else." Angel remembered Gavin always emphasizing the importance of taking care of your team because they were the difference between you winning or losing when it came to business. Angel wanted to continue winning so she had to make sure her team was straight.

"I hope not. Like I said you're one of my best girls. I don't need any of you going anywhere."

What made this batch of women so valuable for Angel was yes they were beautiful and sexy like the other girls that worked for her, but these women understood she was running a business. They conducted themselves like professionals working a job instead of a fun hobby.

Angel loved seeing the enthusiastic expressions on their faces as the girls dined with a five star meal, savored the expensive wine, and chit chatted about what they planned to do with the unexpected extra money they just received.

"Angel, have you thought about what I said," Taren took the opportunity to ask her while the rest of the girls were caught up in their own conversations.

"I have, but are you sure that it's something you really want to do?"

"Yes! I would love to be sitting here counting my two thousand dollar bonus."

"I'm sure you would, but being an escort isn't as easy as you think and definitely not as glamorous. I try to regulate the clients as carefully as possible, but sometimes you get men that nobody would ever want to have sex with, but they've paid for your services and you have to provide them. Because again, this is a business and you have to be professional."

"I get that and I want to do it. I think I can be one of your best girls too."

"Taren, growing up you are always so picky about guys. I mean you did like to have sex, but only with guys you liked and were attracted to. That's not going to always be the case when you're an escort."

"I get that. When I'm working, I'll just pretend like I'm playing a role in a movie. That way when I have to have sex with a guy I'm not attracted to, it's not really me it's my alter ego."

"Whatever works for you."

"Does that mean you're willing to give me a chance?"

"Who am I to deny you the opportunity to

make some good money. As long as you know what you're in for. I just don't want you stepping into something with blinders on."

"I don't. I see clearly."

"Then welcome to Angel's Girls," Angel said, shaking Taren's hand.

"Dawson, I was thrilled when I got your call. We haven't had a chance to hang out in so long," Angel said as the two of them sat outside at a restaurant on Ocean Drive.

"I have football and you're busy being the queen bee. That doesn't leave much free time."

"True, but I'll always make time for you. You're the main reason why my business took off so quickly."

"I plugged you up with some people, but it was your hustler spirit that put it all together. You've established quite the operation. It's very impressive, especially for such a young woman. You've put in a lot of hard work that's why I feel like you deserve to know what is going on behind your back."

"What are you talking about, Dawson?"

Angel questioned putting her fork down.

"A couple of your girls are working side deals with your clients. Instead of going through you, they're having them contact them directly and keeping the money for themselves."

"Are you sure?"

"Positive. One of my boys that booked a girl through your company is the person that told me. He knew you and I were close so he wanted me to know what was going on."

"And what exactly did he tell you?"

"After spending the night with one of your girls she told him if he wanted to see her again to call her directly and she would give him a better rate."

"Are you serious? Which girls?" Angel wanted to know.

"One is a girl named Alicia. But she mentioned to my boy that another girl that worked for you was available in case he had any friends."

"Those scandalous hoes. I bet the other girl is Jessica. Her and Alicia always request to work together whenever possible. I treat my girls so good and this is how they thank me," Angel scoffed, shaking her head in frustration.

"Angel, you know how ruthless it is out here. These girls ain't loyal. All they're interested in is looking out for themselves so be careful," Dawson warned.

"Thank you for bringing this information to me."

"I gotta look out for my girl. I know you'll handle it." Angel nodded her head ready to not only handle the situation, but also let it be known that disloyalty would not be tolerated.

"I know you ladies are wondering why we're having this meeting tonight when you should be working, but something has been brought to my attention and nobody will be working until it's resolved," Angel let it be known. The girls began nervously whispering amongst each other trying to figure out what was going on. "Everyone quiet down," Angel demanded.

"What happened, Angel?" Taren questioned able to see that her friend was very upset.

"It's come to my attention that two women that work for me are cutting side deals with clients behind my back. The problem is I don't know who the girls are," Angel lied. "But until I find out no one will be working."

"Oh hell no! I got too many bills to pay. Whoever the snakes are you need to step forward so we can get back to work," Aspen snapped as she stood up making her position clear.

Angel decided to approach the situation this way because she not only wanted to make sure there was only two snakes in the bunch, she also wanted the other girls to know she could stop them from making money anytime she liked if they crossed her. Putting the spotlight on the incident would help make that possible.

"So nobody wants to step up and take responsibility for their actions," Angel said after no one acknowledged being the guilty party after 15 minutes had passed.

"Maybe someone mistakenly gave you the wrong information, Angel. We all love our job, I don't think any of the girls would risk messing it up," one of the girls said.

"There is no mistake. This is factual information I have. I wouldn't punish all of you if I weren't positive. So either the people responsible will step up or you all can leave now and nobody works."

"Fuck that! Whoever the foul motherfucker is needs to open their mouth and say something. We shouldn't all have to suffer because of your dumbass shit!" another girl yelled.

"She's right. Whoever you are say something! I got daycare bills to pay. Don't nobody have time for this shit!" another girl screamed.

Soon the girls were arguing amongst each other. It was turning into complete chaos. One thing none of the girls wanted was for their money to be fucked up and if they had to rip each other apart to find out who was responsible that's what they planned to do.

"It's Alicia and Jessica!" a voice yelled out from the crowd. At first Angel couldn't see who said it because the way all the women were gathered together.

"Who said that?" Angel questioned loudly.

"Me," Abigail, a tiny Philippine woman raised her hand and said. "It's Jessica and Alicia."

"She's lying," Alicia screamed, jumping towards Abigail, grabbing her hair.

"Get off of me," Abigail cried as Alicia began punching her unmercifully. The other girls had to pull Alicia off of Abigail, as she held her nose trying to stop the bleeding.

"Angel, she lying, I swear!" The scary part was that Alicia sounded as if she was telling the truth. If Angel didn't know otherwise, she may have actually fallen for her wrongly accused act.

"I'm not lying," Abigail said between sniffles. "Her and Jessica came to me trying to see if I wanted to join them. They said I could get a bigger cut and make more money. I told them no."

"They came to me too," another girl Shawna revealed.

"Shut up, Shawna!" Alicia barked.

"Jessica, do you have anything you want to say?" Angel asked.

Jessica glanced over at Alicia who was burning a hole through her chest. Jessica bit down on her bottom lip as if debating what to say. Her hands began shaking nervously.

"Nah, she ain't got nothing to say," Alicia jumped in answering for Jessica.

"Let Jessica speak for herself," Angel said, folding her arms.

"I'm sorry, Angel. You've been so good to me, to all of us and you didn't deserve for us to betray you," Jessica said putting her head down in shame.

"You greedy bitches," Aspen said shaking her head. "Now you not gon' have shit."

"Disloyalty will never be tolerated within my organization. Jessica, Alicia, Abigail and Shawna, you are all fired."

"Why me and Abigail? We didn't do anything," Shawna cried.

"Precisely, you didn't do anything. Both of you should have come to me as soon as you were aware that Jessica and Alicia were partaking in shady dealings."

"But…"

"But nothing," Angel said cutting Shawna off. "You can only pick one side, there is no fence walking over here. You and Abigail picked your side when you decided to keep Jessica and Alicia's secret. I want the four of you to leave now and if anybody else is even considering following in their footsteps you need to leave with them. This is a warning to all of you, nobody better fuck with me, or you will be dismissed."

Chapter Seventeen

'Bout My Paper

Darien Blaze got up from one of the booths he had in the VIP section, with a magnum bottle of Ace Of Spades Rose in one hand, to jump on the mic at the nightclub. He gave not one fuck that the DJ was in the middle of playing a record, or that he was about to introduce a new song by an artist who just finished performing at the club. In his mind, none of that mattered because he was Darien Blaze, the undisputed welterweight champion of the world.

Darien had the entire VIP section blocked off for him and his entourage. They were still celebrating his win from a week ago. They had moved the party from Las Vegas to Miami and planned on being in New York for part three tomorrow night. As he arrogantly took over the DJ booth, he relished being in the spotlight until someone caught his attention. He wasn't sure if it was the way the lights flickered off her skin in the slinky short dress she was wearing, or the way the front of her jet black hair swooped across her right eye but Darien was captivated.

No longer interested in taking over as DJ, Darien quickly dropped the mic, brushed passed his bodyguards and got to his right hand man Kaleb.

"You see that young lady over there in the silver dress," Darien said, pointing to the woman he planned on taking home tonight.

"Yep, what about her?" Kaleb asked.

"Give her these two bottles of Ace Of Spades. Tell her it's a gift for her and her girlfriends from me. Then let her know I'll like to meet her," Darien explained.

"Got you! I'll be right back," Kaleb said taking the bottles and heading towards the women. "Excuse me, Miss," he said to the woman Darien was interested in. "My man over there wanted me to give you these bottles."

"For what? I don't need his bottles," Angel snapped and turned back around to continue talking to Aspen, Taren, and Laurie.

Kaleb tapped Angel on the shoulder and at first she ignored him until he tapped again. "It's a gift and he would like to meet you," Kaleb stated once he had her attention again.

"Dude listen. I'm not interested in your friend and I'm definitely not interested in these little bottles of champagne."

"Yo' shorty, this is Ace Of Spades. You know how much a bottle of this shit cost," Kaleb shot back.

"Yeah, too much in the fuckin' club for what you pay at the damn store. Plus that bullshit only cost $13 a bottle to make. So what's your point... that your man likes to waste money? Like I said, I'm not interested so carry on," Angel said shooing Kaleb away.

Kaleb stood staring Angel up and down for a minute baffled by her attitude. Any second he was expecting her to turn around and say she was just playing, but when that didn't happen he had to deal with the fact he was shut down and that was something completely new to him.

"She must have a man or something because she said she wasn't interested," Kaleb informed

Darien once he made it back over to the VIP section.

"What do you mean she's not interested? Did you offer her the bottles of champagne?"

"Yes and she said she didn't want them."

"Did you tell her I wanted to meet her?"

"Told her that too and she said she wasn't interested."

"You must've misunderstood," Darien said not believing that any woman would turn down his advances. "Let me go over there."

"Darien, let it go," Kaleb said putting his hand on his man's shoulder. "There are other girls in this club, shit five came wit' you. No need to bother yourself wit' someone that's not trying to be down wit' the team."

Before Kaleb could say another word, Darien was making a beeline in Angel's direction. His security team were right on his ass to guarantee nothing happened to the money making machine. At first Angel didn't notice what looked like a mob of people heading towards her until Aspen got her attention.

"Girl, Darien Blaze is coming straight for you," Aspen gasped.

"Who the fuck is Darien Blaze and why does that name sound so familiar?" she questioned, feeling irritated that the answer hadn't come to her.

"The boxer Darien Blaze. Everybody knows who he is," Laurie chimed in. "Everybody except for you I guess." She laughed.

"That's right. He's the reason business was slow last weekend because everybody was in Vegas for the fight. They didn't need any of my girls with all that endless pussy for sale," Angel huffed; thinking how pissed off she was that the fight put a minor dent in her pockets. Angel wasn't able to think about being upset much longer because next thing she knew Darien was in her face.

"I wanted to come over and introduce myself. I'm Darien Blaze and you are..." Darien had his hand extended. Angel felt some type of way this man was putting her on the spot in the middle of the club. It didn't help matters that he had about four big ass bodyguards with him. She felt he was making a spectacle of himself and she wanted no part of it.

"I appreciate you offering the bottles of champagne and nothing against you, but like I told your friend, I'm not interested," Angel said trying to be somewhat polite. She had reminded herself that she did run an escort service that catered to rich men like Darien. Even if she had no interest in him personally, Angel didn't want to burn any bridges in case they decided to do business in the future.

"Is there a reason why you're not interested in me?" Darien asked point blank. His directness threw Angel off.

"I didn't know I needed a reason," she countered.

"I'm trying to understand why you wouldn't be interested in me. I have everything going for myself. Unless you already have a man, but even then, he couldn't be a better fit for you then me."

Angel burst out laughing unable to hide how lame she thought he sounded. "I apologize, I didn't mean to laugh in your face like that, but ummm were you serious with that comment or was it a joke?"

"I was serious... very serious. That's how confident I am in myself."

"All that sounds good, but like I said I'm not interested. Now if you'll excuse me I want to get back to talking to my friends."

"I'll let you go for now, but we'll be back in touch. And when I finally make you mine I won't hold it against you that you wasted so much time," Darien said, before walking off.

"Yo, that man's ego is out of this world," Angel said when he left.

"He has every right to be. He's one of the highest paid athletes in the world. He wouldn't have gotten there if he didn't have that ego," Aspen reasoned.

"I'm trying to understand why you didn't give him any play," Taren jumped in and said. "You already know if that nigga would've stepped to me, I'd been like deuces to you bitches."

"Me too." Laurie smiled.

"You already know I would've been," Aspen added.

"Besides the fact his over-inflated ego rubbed me the wrong way, reason number two is because I'm sure he has at least a dozen chicks just like the three of you already in the mix and that's only his main chicks. I'm not even including the side chicks, the side side chicks, and the one-night stands. Don't nobody have time to deal with the headaches that come with entertaining fools like that," Angel spat.

"With all the money he got, I would have to make an exception to every rule," Taren said as Aspen and Laurie both cosigned.

"Good for the three of you. Now let's go get some drinks and start partying before I get bored and say let's go," Angel cracked, leading the ladies to the bar.

Darien watched Angel from a short distance interacting with her girlfriends. He hadn't been rejected in any sector of his life in so long that you would think Darien would be angry with Angel for shutting him down, but instead it made him more determined to win her over. Like most athletes who excel on a high level, they're always chasing the win, and the win so happens to be whatever it is they are playing for at the time. For Darien, Angel had now become the chase and he would hunt her down until he got the win.

"I can't believe you're going to this game and I can't believe I let you drag my ass with you," Angel said as they headed towards the American Airlines Arena.

"I couldn't pass up no good seats to the Heat game and they playing Oklahoma too. My boo hooked me up. I'ma be cheering for him so hard during the game," Aspen bragged looking in the passenger mirror as she applied Mac Snob lipstick.

"Bitch, you so messy. I'm telling you now. If that nigga's baby mama walk up on you, don't think I'm about to step in and even break a nail to defend you when she start whooping yo' ass," Angel scoffed.

"Her silly ass ain't gon' do shit. She already know what it is. Hell, she used to be in my position before she got knocked up. I guess she figured a baby would make her the official girl and slow his ass down... not! That's why I play my position, get the money and perks, and enjoy it while it last because I know it ain't."

"You don't have to school me to the game 'cause I'm the one that taught you, but you still messy as fuck. But this is going to be a good game so my ass is willing to let you be messy so shame on me too." Angel smiled then both of the women started laughing.

"But wait, let me tell you what happened when—"

"Hold that thought," Angel said cutting Aspen off. "Let me take this call," she said, answering the phone she handled business on. "Hello."

"Yes, I got your card from a business acquaintance. I was told you had the best girls in the city," the male caller said.

"That's correct which means they cost top dollar."

"No problem. My client is having a private party after the game tonight and wanted ten of your best girls to be there for the night."

"When you say for the night do you mean all night?"

"Yes, if possible."

"Anything is possible for the right price," Angel stated.

"Name the price."

"Ten girls all night, one hundred thousand," Angel said without flinching. When Aspen heard the number that came out of Angel's mouth, she stopped primping in the mirror and looked at her with a what the fuck look.

"Done," he said. Angel winked her eye at Aspen and gave a thumbs up after the man agreed to her price.

"I only accept cash and I must have it in advance before any of my girls step foot in the party."

"Let me know the time and location and I'll be there with the money."

"Cool, I'll be in touch," Angel said and ended the call.

"Bitch, did you just score a hundred g's for ten girls! How in the fuck!" Aspen screamed in excitement.

"I don't know, it was just a couple of key words he said that made me feel like I could get the money so I went for it."

"Key words like what?"

"Private party, game, heard you gave the best girls in the city... shit like that. Then when he requested an all-nighter, I knew it was time to go hard."

"Yo, I better be one of those ten girls to work that gig tonight," Aspen demanded.

"You not hanging out with your basketball boo after the game?"

"Girl, he can wait. I ain't getting no g's outta him tonight. His baby mama can have him."

"I ain't gon' never stop you from getting your paper. One girl down, nine more to go. Now let's go enjoy this basketball game before we get this paper tonight," Angel smiled pressing down on the gas pedal.

Chapter Eighteen

Came Back For You

When Angel arrived at the meeting location to pick up the money, per usual she had Gunner with her in case things got ugly. She learned from Gavin that you could never be too careful when it comes to your money. Angel walked towards the parked limo with Gunner not far behind, armed and ready to fire if need be. As Angel got closer, the back window slowly went down.

"Oh hell no!" Angel barked. "I know you didn't call wasting my motherfuckin' time," she spit. "Gunner, let's get the fuck outta here."

"You leaving before getting your money," Darien said, flashing the stacks of cash.

Angel stopped in her tracks. She eyed Darien and then the cash. "So this is legit? You do want the 10 girls for a party tonight?"

"Sure do. I was supposed to be in NYC tonight, but decided to stay for you."

"I need my money."

"Here it is," Darien said, handing her the cash.

"Gunner, count this for me," Angel said, tossing the envelope full of money to him. "Your 10 girls will be at the address given to me at 10 o'clock," Angel informed Darien. "It was nice doing business with you. If you have any problems with the girls' services feel free to give me a call."

"Wait... wait... wait!" Darien yelled out the window. "I just dropped one hundred stacks and that's all I get?"

"You paid for some prime pussy and I'm delivering it to you so you're getting exactly what you paid for."

"No, I'm not because I'm not getting you."

"I'm not for sale, but even if I was, I would cost a lot more than a hundred thousand dollars."

"I'm not trying to buy you with that hundred thousand, that ain't nothing. You're a businesswoman; I'm simply making a contribution to your cause. I respect a woman with her own hustle. But as a good paying customer, I think you could show me a little love." Darien smiled.

"What kind of love are you looking for?"

"How about you be my special guest at the party tonight."

"I don't attend parties my girls are working. It's not good for business."

"I don't have to go to the party. Those girls aren't for me anyway. I much rather spend my evening with you."

"No, I want you at the party. In case anything happens I like for the paying customer to be in the vicinity."

"What about dinner tomorrow night?"

"Lunch," Angel countered.

"How about lunch and dinner."

"Lunch and then lose my number, unless of course you wanna do more business. Take it or leave it."

"I'll see you tomorrow for lunch," Darien said rolling the window up before the limo drove off.

Angel stood in front of the floor length mirror in her bedroom dissecting the outfit she chose to wear for her lunch with Darien. She thought the Gucci peach silk Georgette jumpsuit with crystal studs and nude Christian Louboutin pumps gave the look she was going for, very casual but sexy at the same time.

She didn't want to admit it, but Angel was looking forward to her lunch with Darien. His overconfident disposition was a bit of a turnoff, but there was something about him that sparked Angel's interest.

Angel arrived at the Azul restaurant inside of the Mandarin Oriental Hotel. Darien was already seated and Angel noticed his bodyguards were sitting two tables away.

"I was worried you weren't going to show," Darien said, standing up and pulling out the chair so Angel could sit down.

"I'm a woman of my word."

"I believe that."

"I heard your party was a huge success. My girls had nothing bad to report."

"Did they tell you that I didn't touch any of them? I slept alone last night."

"I didn't ask and I hope you didn't sleep alone to impress me."

"That's the only reason I slept alone. Don't tell me it was a waste."

"Unfortunately it was. But you live and learn. The good news is today is another day, so you can make up for last night."

"The only thing I want is you. That's it," Darien stated.

"I can't lie, that aggressive, I won't take no for an answer attitude you have is rather appealing, but in the business I'm in, I deal with men like you all the time. You're all players with out of this world egos and you juggle too many women to keep track of. I don't need that sort of stress in my life. Running a business full of high-strung females is enough hassle."

"How did you become involved in the escort business?"

"I was a college student looking for a way to make some extra money. I knew some hot girls that loved to have sex. I figured if they were doing it for free, why not help them get paid and I make a financial come up at the same time."

"You seem to be doing well for yourself."

"I am. Once I got my girls to understand

they were getting paid to leave and not to stay, business started booming."

"So did you start off as an escort yourself?"

"Never."

"Why not?"

"Honestly, I'm still a virgin," Angel admitted. Angel thought Darien was going to spit out his water when she told him that. The expression on his face was priceless.

"Stop lying."

"I'm not lying, it's true."

"How old are you?"

"Twenty."

"A 20-year-old virgin who is beautiful and sexy, never thought I would see the day."

"It's not that big of a deal. I've been caught up in making money since I was 14 years old so I never had time to even think about entertaining a relationship. Time kept passing and here I am."

"Here you are. Right where you're supposed to be, with me."

"You think so."

"I know so. You can imagine how many women I've had access to, but I was so drawn to you. It's more than just your outward appearance. You give off this energy that's contagious. Come to New York with me. We'll only be there for a couple days. I'll get you your own hotel room."

"I don't know."

"Have you ever been to New York?"

"No, I haven't."

"Let your first time be with me. I can show you the city. We'll have a good time. I promise," he said, reaching over the table and putting his hand on top of Angel's.

"Why not. A girl does need to live a little, right?"

"My point exactly." Darien grinned.

"New York here I come."

Chapter Nineteen

Untouchable

Darien Blaze was known to the world as a man who had it all; fame, wealth, and the undisputed champ. He lived the sort of jet set life that many dreamed of, but few ever got a glimpse. He was born and raised in the South Bronx zip code of 10451. One of the poorest zip codes in America. The majority of children there grew up in subsidized housing, raised in poverty in single parent homes. Darien grew up under the same conditions, except he was born with a gift of speed, strength, and most importantly determination. That determination turned Darien Blaze into one of the richest athletes in the world. But with all his money and fame Darien couldn't leave the streets behind. His addiction to illegal activities gave him a high that not even a championship belt could contain.

"My man, Nico Carter. As always it's good to see you," Darien said, shaking Nico's hand when he entered his house.

"It's good to see you too, Mr. Blaze." Nico laughed.

"I was disappointed you and Genesis didn't make it to Vegas for my fight."

"I know. We wanted to, but business got the best of us. You know how that goes," Nico said directing Darien to his office. "Now what can I do for one of my best clients?" Nico questioned, closing the door behind them.

"I need to place an order, but I need more product this time."

"We got you covered. Let me know how much and when you need it."

"I appreciate that. We've been doing business for a long time now and you always look out."

"Always will. Although I still don't understand with all the millions you make why you still move these drugs."

"Man, it's hard giving up all that tax free money. Plus, it keeps my boys eatin' good and the hoods loving me. What can I say, I love to be loved." Darien smiled.

"I feel you. So how long will you be in New York?"

"Just a few days. I brought my lady friend. I'ma show her around the city. You should come out with us. Bring somebody and we can make it a double date."

"I appreciate the invite and I would take you up on your offer but I'm actually about to catch a flight. I have to make a trip to LA for a couple days. But next time for sure."

"No doubt. I'm not gonna hold you up, man. I'll be looking out for my product."

"I'll be in touch. Talk to you soon," Nico said walking Darien out.

Nico did genuinely like Darien, but felt he needed to keep him somewhat at arm's length. Nico thought Darien was cool, but knew he surrounded himself with a reckless crew. His entourage didn't mean any harm they just didn't know any better. But because Darien had this need to appease them, in the back of Nico's mind there was always some concern his crew would do some dumb shit to fuck everything up and Nico didn't want no part of it. Not only that because of Darien's overly confident sense of security, he believed he was untouchable and Nico was well aware that in his line of business, everyone could be touched including Darien.

"You look gorgeous," Darien, said when Angel opened her hotel room door. She was wearing a DSquared2 electric blue snakeskin dress with matching stilettos. Her long black hair was in a high bun highlighting her diamond hoop earrings.

"I'm glad you approve."

"I more than approve. You ready to go?"

"Yep, let me get my purse. You still haven't told me where we're going."

"It's a surprise," Darien said studying every curve on Angel's body as she went to retrieve her purse.

"Did I tell you I don't like surprises? "

"No you didn't and even if you don't like surprises, you're going to love mine," Darien said with confidence.

Before Angel knew it they had arrived on the West Side and were being whisked away in an awaiting helicopter. Their destination was the Hamptons where Darien had prepared a candlelight dinner at an oceanfront estate.

"This is beautiful. But I have to wonder how many other women you've used this ruse on."

"None, only because they've never required it of me. I haven't had to put work into a woman in a very long time."

"Really... so you call this putting in work. So you know this is only the beginning. You have a lot more to do," Angel teased.

"I'm ready. I love a challenge. The more work the greater the reward.

"And so the challenge begins." Angel smiled, raising her champagne glass.

Chapter Twenty

I Love You... I Love You Too

After Angel's trip to New York with Darien they began a whirlwind romance that went from zero to sixty in an instant. Instead of Darien going back to his main residence in Las Vegas he stayed at his luxury condo in Miami so he could be near Angel. They were spending every day and night together. Angel brought out Darien's laidback, loving side and he brought out her fun, adventurous side so they complemented one another.

"Girl, if this dude has anymore flowers delivered to your crib, this place is going to start looking like a garden. Does he send them every day, damn," Aspen said placing the bouquet that was just delivered on the kitchen table.

"He's so romantic." Angel blushed, smelling the flowers.

"Girl, you is really smitten with this dude. I never thought I would see the day that a guy would be able to get you to blush. For a minute I started thinking you might not even be interested in men," Aspen joked sitting down on the couch.

"You know with the business we're in, it doesn't exactly give you the best impression of men. You know I had no intention of even dating Darien let alone falling in love," Angel caught herself as soon as the words came out of her mouth.

"In love. Did I hear you correctly? Did you say you're in love with Darien?"

"I can't believe I said that either. I guess I am in love."

"Girl, that ain't love you just dick whipped, that's all," Aspen reasoned.

"You can't be dick whipped over a man you've never had sex with."

"Wait, you and Darien Blaze have never had sex?"

"Nope."

"Bitch, you are good. I think that's an excellent game you've been playing wit' that nigga. Keep dangling the possibility of him getting the pussy while he continues to trick on you. At this rate you might get a couple cars and crib out the deal."

"Aspen, it's not about that. This isn't a game. The last few months we've really had an opportunity to get to know each other. Instead of having sex all the time we're talking and laughing all the time, we've become friends so when we do become lovers there will be a genuine connection."

"Well damn, I never thought about that."

"Of course you haven't because getting men to spend their money on you is what you do. But I'm not knocking your hustle. You better get it while you can because you never know when that shit will come to a halt," Angel said, before reading a text on her phone.

"Don't you think I know it? That's why I be trying to work as much as possible. Those gigs haven't been coming nonstop like they used to," Aspen smacked. "You done fell in love and forgot about your girls."

"Nah, I haven't forgotten about my girls. I will admit that I've been slacking lately, not on top of business like I used to, but I have some work for you tonight if you want it."

"Hell yeah I want it!"

"Cool, I just got a text he needs two girls for three hours. Do you want to use Laurie?"

"Most definitely because she needs the money and I don't want her slacking on her portion of the bills. So yes, let's use Laurie."

"That works. I will send you all the information. But it's for nine o'clock tonight."

"Perfect. That gives me enough time to get my hair done, a wax, and all the cute shit," Aspen said, reaching for her purse and cell phone before standing up.

"I know I was giving you a little hard time about business, but I'm really happy for you. Falling in love has made you loosen up a lot. It's nice seeing that side of you."

"Me too. Now get outta here. I don't want any excuses. I do not want you being late for the client. You know how I hate tardiness so be on time."

"I got you boss."

Right after Aspen left she saw a text come through from Darien that put a smile on her face.

I can't wait to see you tonight, it said. Angel was looking forward to seeing him too. So much so that she thought tonight might be the night they went further than foreplay. Angel had even purchased a wicked rose colored lace crisscross babydoll lingerie, that had a revealing flyaway back, sheer skirt and matching v-string panty. Angel knew Darien would be more interested in taking off the lingerie than seeing her in it, but for her the teasing would be the funniest part.

"I just saw you yesterday and I was still missing you," Darien said when he opened the door giving Angel a kiss.

"I was missing you too. So much so that instead of us going out why don't we stay in. I don't want to share you tonight."

"Are you sure? You look so good tonight I want to show you off," Darien said, kissing Angel's neck.

"You look good too," she commented, liking his Balmain Moto Jeans with a crisp white button shoulder stripe t-shirt that complimented his perfectly sculptured biceps. "I'm just not in the mood to be bothered will all the people that will be coming up asking for your autograph," Angel complained.

"You're gonna have to get used to that. It comes with the territory being my girl."

"I know and I can deal with it, but tonight I want it to be just us. Is that okay?"

"That's more than okay. We can watch a movie and order pizza," Darien said as they headed towards the living room. " But before we do that, there is something I wanted to discuss with you anyway."

"You sound serious."

"It is serious."

"What?"

"I want us to move in together and before you go saying you don't think we know each other well enough, what better way to get to know somebody then to move in with each other. But real talk, I feel like I've known you forever. I think we would be good."

"I feel the same way, but my concern is are you sure you're ready for such a huge step. I mean you're known for your bachelor lifestyle."

"I can't be a bachelor forever now can I."

"You want us to move in together even though we haven't had sex yet?"

"I tasted it so I know the sex is gonna be good. So I ain't worried." Darien gave a devilish smile.

"You're the worst," Angel said, hitting him

with a pillow from the couch. "I do have an issue about something."

"Tell me."

"This was your bachelor pad. I'm assuming you want me to move in with you since my loft is super cute for me, but I know your taste is much more extravagant."

"True... true," he agreed.

"The thing is, I know you've had a slew of chicks come through here and I don't want to make this my home."

"We'll pick out a new house together. Problem solved."

"You don't mind?"

"Not at all. It'll be nice starting fresh with you."

"So you sure you want to do this?" Angel questioned wanting further confirmation.

"Positive. I've been thinking about it for a while. I was gonna ask as soon as we got back from New York, but I thought that was rushing it a little too much. But I'm ready. What about you?"

"So am I. I'm ready for something else too," Angel leaned over and kissed Darien.

"I been ready," Darien said reciprocating the kiss with even more intensity. He reached for the waist-defining belt on Angel's honey-colored Burberry Buckingham double-breasted cotton trench coat. "So this is what you were hiding under this coat," Darien said, taking in the sexy lingerie Angel was wearing.

"I told you I was ready," Angel said straddling Darien. He slid the strap down on her lingerie, exposing her full breasts. His hands caressed Angel's firm round ass while his tongue made its way to her hardened nipples as he took turns licking each one. The moistness of Darien's mouth had Angel's body tingling. She could feel her pussy getting wet although she hadn't even felt the tip of his dick inside of her yet.

"I can't wait to make love to you," Darien whispered in Angel's ear before lifting her up and taking her to his bedroom. He continued to sprinkle her neck and chest with passionate kisses until laying her down on his bed. Darien slowly removed the rose-colored babydoll lingerie and stared at Angel's naked body. It seemed to be illuminating because of the moonlight shining through the glass and accentuating every curve on her body.

"You have no idea how much I want to feel you inside of me," Angel purred, going over to Darien as he began undressing. When he took off his t-shirt, Angel reached her hand out and let her fingers glide across every inch of his chest. It seemed to be like a maze with all the muscle definition. When Darien unzipped his jeans and he was fully undressed, his body resembled a pure bred flawless black stallion. Darien kept himself together like a well-oiled machine and Angel yearned to know exactly what that felt like.

Darien's dick was so hard he wanted to instantly slide inside and soak in Angel's wet juices, but knowing that she was a virgin, he had to exercise self control and slow down. Instead, Darien glided his hands up Angel's legs and thighs until grasping her ass in his large hands. He brought her sugar walls to his mouth letting his tongue devour her clit.

"Oh, Darien. Oh, Darien," Angel called out as she looked down to watch his tongue make love to her pussy. Each movement was deliberate with meaning and before long her pussy began to tighten up and the wetness increased. A tingle slowly shot through her body getting stronger and stronger with every stroke of Darien's tongue. Angel thought she was on her way to heaven when her body shivered uncontrollably after experiencing her very first orgasm.

"Put it in," she begged wanting the magical sensation to continue. Angel's sexual desire had reached a peak and now she craved more. Darien took his time, gently sliding inch by inch of his long thick dick inside of her still dripping wet pussy. The deeper Darien went the louder Angel's screams became until they turned into soft cries.

"Oh, baby I love you," Darien whispered in Angel's ear, as his mind, body and soul became completely enthralled in making love to her.

"I love you too," Angel whispered back.

After they finished making love for what seemed like eternity, Darien held Angel close in his arms wanting to keep her body near him.

"You feel so warm," Angel said lovingly. "Being in your arms feels almost as good as you did inside of me.

"This used to be the part of sex I always avoided. I never wanted the intimacy, but with you it feels so right, like I'm exactly where I'm supposed to be," Darien said, kissing the back of Angel's neck.

"That's because you are." Angel smiled.

"I agree. What's this on the back of your neck?" Darien questioned as he continued sprinkling more kisses.

"You're talking about that teardrop, it's my birthmark."

"It's very distinctive, but cute on you. Did you inherit it from your mother or father? One of my cousins has a unique birthmark that he inherited from his mother. Is there something wrong?" Darien asked feeling Angel's body tense up.

"We've talked about so much, but never my parents," Angel said softly.

"Is there a reason for that? Are you not close to them?"

"My mother died giving birth to me and she never told anybody who my father was, so I have no idea who he is. My grandmother raised me, but two years ago she died of a heart attack."

"Baby, I'm so sorry. I had no idea you suffered so many loses," Darien said holding Angel even tighter.

"Thank you."

"But you have me now baby, and I'm never going to leave you," Darien promised.

Hearing Darien say those words gave Angel the sense of love and security her heart always yearned for, but never thought possible.

Chapter Twenty-One

Tragedy

Darien was on his way to pick up the keys to the new house he purchased for him and Angel. He never imagined he would meet a woman that would even make him consider settling down, but Angel—she was different. She had this fire that burned inside of her that Darien was so drawn to. And after that night they made love, Darien was more sure than ever that Angel was the only woman for him. Now that they had found the perfect house Darien felt it was only a matter of time before they would be ready to start a family. While Darien was thinking about what their kids would look like and what they would name them he saw Nico calling. "Nico Carter, what can I do for you?" Darien said when he answered.

"My man, Darien. I was beginning to feel as if you were avoiding my calls. I've left you messages; I don't get a call back. I don't want to believe that a man I've been doing business with for a long time would be trying to curve me. Is that what's going on, Darien?"

"Now why would I do that? Like you said we've been doing business for years."

"Maybe because you have an outstanding bill with me," Nico countered. "A bill that is long overdue. That's not how we conduct business. I thought we was better than that."

"About that bill. I won't be paying it."

"Excuse me, I don't think I heard you correctly. I'm sure you didn't say that you're not going to pay the money you owe me."

"Nico, the thing is my boys told me that the last shipment was a bad batch and they couldn't make no money from it. You can't expect me to pay for something my crew couldn't eat off of."

"Darien, when have I ever given you a bad batch of anything?" Nico questioned trying to remain calm. "If you had a problem with my product you should've stepped to me immediately."

"We all make mistakes sometimes."

"I don't make those type of mistakes. With most of our clients we get paid once the product is in your hand. Last few times I made an exception with you because we have history. Don't make me regret that decision."

"My man, I ain't trying to make you regret nothing. But like I said, yo' shit was bad. My boys ain't got to lie about that."

"I tell you what, Darien, just give me the product back. You keep your money, I keep my product, problem solved."

"I can check with my boys, but I doubt they still have the product. You know how it go, Nico. We've always done good business together and I want it to continue, but like I said I can't pay for something my boys couldn't make no money on."

"Darien, I don't give a fuck what yo' boys said. You either give me back my money or my product. The choice is yours, but you need to make it quickly. I'll be in touch," Nico said before ending the call.

Angel was listening to her favorite Rihanna CD and packing up her clothes when she noticed Aspen calling her. She turned down the loud music and answered her phone.

"Hey Aspen, what's up?"

"It's Laurie," Aspen said sounding hysterical. "She's in the emergency room."

"Text me the information. I'm on the way," Angel said grabbing her purse and car keys and rushing out.

Angel was pushing 100 as she sped to the hospital. She was lucky she didn't get pulled over by the cops or worse, get in an accident and kill herself or somebody else. When she got inside, Aspen and Taren were both there with the look of dread on their faces.

"Tell me what happened?" Angel asked out of breath from running as fast as she could.

"A customer did this to her," Aspen said, barely holding it together.

"What are you talking about? Her last customer was last night."

"The cleaning lady at the hotel didn't find

her body until this morning."

"This can't be happening," Angel said, taking a seat. "Is she going to be okay?"

"I don't know. He beat her pretty badly. I didn't even recognize her. They put her in an induced coma until the swelling around her brain went down," Aspen cried.

"Laurie will pull through," Taren said, rubbing Aspen's shoulder.

Angel scrolled through her phone to see who was the client Laurie saw last night. The name was Stephen Marks and he was a first time customer. Everything seemed to be legit with him, but clearly Angel had dropped the ball and sent Laurie to meet a monster.

"Laurie is strong, she'll pull through," Angel said reassuring Aspen and Taren before going in the room to see Laurie.

"I hope she's right," Aspen said to Taren wiping away her tears.

When Angel entered Laurie's room she didn't know what to expect. But she wasn't prepared for just how bruised and battered her face was. Laurie was hooked up to all sorts of tubes and her body was completely motionless. Angel stroked Laurie's hair as a tear dropped from her eye.

"Laurie, I'm so, so sorry. This should have never happened to you. You don't deserve to be in this hospital room. I don't know what sort of monster would do something like this, but he will pay, that I can promise you. I don't care what I have to do, or how long it takes but I will track the animal down and make sure he's never able to hurt another woman again."

Chapter Twenty-Two

Scheming

Nico stood in his Miami penthouse, staring out the massive window at the ocean view. It was another beautiful day in the city, but only darkness was looming over Nico's thoughts. Tonight he would make his move and it would either get Nico what he wanted or it would be the beginning of endless bloodshed.

"Nico, our men are in place ready to move," Elijah stated, snapping Nico out of his thoughts.

"Good. I'm gonna give Darien one more

opportunity to make shit right, if not then the bodies will start dropping. Starting with his woman," Nico said turning back around, soaking in the majestic view.

"Baby, you ready for tonight," Darien said, kissing Angel's neck.

"You know I am. I can't wait for this so-called surprised birthday party you planned for me," she giggled.

"The party is just the beginning. Wait 'til you see the real surprise," Darien baited.

"What is it? Tell me, I want to know," Angel beamed, following Darien out of the bathroom.

"I'm not telling you now. Then it wouldn't be a surprise. But trust me, you gon' love it. Only the best for my baby girl."

"Damn! Tonight can't get here fast enough," Angel said stepping into the His and Her walk-in master closet to look at her birthday dress.

"So that's what you wearing tonight... nice," Darien commented walking past her on the way back into the bathroom.

"Yeah, but I can't decide what shoes I'm going

to wear. None of them seem to be screaming out to me," Angel said looking at the rows of designer shoes on the two-tone glass shelves.

"Go buy some more," Darien said, pulling out a wad of money and handing it to Angel.

"A little shopping therapy is always good for the soul." She laughed, laying the money on the island in the center of the closet that was the size of a huge bedroom.

"Today is your day... well everyday is your day, but today is even more special because this is the day you were brought into this world. I want you to have everything your heart desires and then some." Darien smiled, kissing Angel on the lips. Angel took it a step further, pressing her tongue down his throat before slowly licking around his lips.

"You shouldn't have started something I can't finish," she teased sliding her hand down his pants.

"What you mean? I got time," Darien said, pulling Angel close.

"I can't be late for my hair appointment," Angel said between kisses. "But I'll make it up to you tonight. It will be my gift to you."

"So you giving out presents on your birthday. I'm a lucky man."

"Yes, you are Darien Blaze." Angel kissed her

man one more time before grabbing her purse and money, then leaving.

Angel pulled out the front gates in her pearl white Aston Martin unaware that every move she made was being monitored. Angel was too focused on the fact that for the first time in the last three months she wasn't dealing with drama. The incident with Laurie had totally devastated Angel. For a minute she even contemplated getting out the business for good. It shook her confidence that she sent one of her girls to a client that almost killed her. Luckily, Laurie survived but she would never be the same again.

The main reason Angel didn't close shop was because so many of the girls relied on her for work. She didn't want them to suffer because she felt guilty over what happened to Laurie. Instead she tightened up her screening process for clients even more and paid for all her girls to take self-defense classes. So with how rough things had been lately this birthday party Darien was giving her was exactly what Angel needed.

"Angel's party is going to be everything tonight.

And you know Darien is going to have all his baller friends up in that club. We have to make sure we are extra on point tonight," Aspen smacked, as her and Taren strolled through the mall trying to find something to wear.

"Yeah, I'm sure it will be cool," Taren said nonchalantly. "It ain't like we haven't been to nice parties before," Taren huffed.

"Girl, you know this party gon' be the bomb. Stop acting like you ain't excited," Aspen commented while walking, before slowing down and glancing over at Taren. "Am I sensing an attitude with you. What's really going on?"

Taren sighed and huffed some more before finally speaking. "I mean, aren't you tired of following behind Angel?"

"Where is this coming from?" Aspen questioned, puzzled by Taren's comment.

"It just seems to me that ever since Angel got with Darien she act like she better than us."

"Nah, why would you even say that? That's supposed to be your girl. Ya supposed to be best friends."

"Look, all I'm saying is that shit done changed with Angel lately. She used to keep us working, but it's like she don't even have time to run the business no more," Taren popped. "And we can't forget what happened to Laurie."

"We can't blame Angel for that," Aspen said in a serious tone. "There are psychos everywhere and unfortunately Laurie came in contact with one. In the business we're in that's always a possibility. Luckily Laurie survived her nightmare."

"I hear you, but I don't think the girls or her business is a priority any longer," Taren stated.

"I mean she is in a serious relationship now. It's a little hard for her to book clients while she's traveling around with her man. But I'm happy for her."

"Happy for her?" Taren frowned.

"For sure. Ever since I met Angel she has been hustling to make that money, now she got a man that can give her everything she wants. Shiiit, I'm tryna be like Angel," Aspen said snapping her fingers doing a little two step dance.

"We can have what Angel has and make it even better," Taren said matter of factly. Aspen just looked at Taren in dismay. "We can take over her escort service and make the business even more lucrative."

"Taren, what the hell are you talkin' about. First of all, Angel would never let us take over a business that she built and even if we wanted to we don't have access to all her millionaire clients. We could never make it work. You remember what happened to Jessica, Alicia, Shawna and

Abigail. They are probably somewhere working a street corner."

"What if we could? What if I not only had access to all her biggest clients, but I also had someone that was willing to bring in even more ballers who would pay big money for our company services."

"Girl, you are really serious about this," Aspen said shaking her head. "I'm telling you now to dead the idea before you end up dead, literally after Angel finds out what you scheming on and kills yo' ass," Aspen warned.

"I'm not worried about Angel. I don't think she'll be around much longer to run the business anyway." Taren shrugged.

"What do you mean by that? Is there something you know that you're not telling me?" Aspen wanted to know.

"I'm just saying, things happen. What happened to Laurie is a perfect example of that. You never know. One day a person seems to have it all and then the next...." Taren's voice trailed off without finishing her sentence.

Aspen brushed off what Taren said as her being an envious friend doing some wishful thinking. She felt Taren was harmless and honestly understood why she would have some jealously towards Angel, all of them did, but it was more admiration than anything else. Angel was a bonafied hustler and about her business. She played no games when it came to making money. While the other girls were partying, Angel was somewhere trying to close a deal that would bring in more money not only for herself, but for the girls that worked for her. They respected and loved her and so did Taren, or at least that was what Aspen thought.

Chapter Twenty-Three

Part Of Me

"Babe, I'm on my way home now," Angel said as soon as she answered the phone. When she saw Darien's number pop up she knew he was calling checking on her whereabouts.

"Cool. Hurry, baby. I got something here waiting for you."

"What, like a pre-present before the real present," Angel joked.

"Yeah, I guess you can call it that. Now get yo' ass home," Darien laughed before hanging up.

As Angel was putting her bags in the trunk of her car she heard her cell ringing again and immediately answered the phone thinking it was Darien calling back. "Yes, babe?"

"Nah, it ain't yo' boo."

"Hey, girl. What's up?" Angel said, putting her last bag in the trunk.

"Where are you?" Taren asked, pulling on a blunt.

"Leaving Bal Harbour."

"I bet you got yourself something cute," Taren said rolling her eyes, disguising her jealously with a sweet happy tone.

"I got a few things. Way more than I planned. But Darien said it was my day and I should not be denied." Angel smiled. "He's such a sweetie."

"Yeah, he is. You're lucky to have him and he's just as lucky to have you too."

"Thanks, Taren. I do feel lucky. But what's up with you? You ready for tonight?"

"Girl, I was on my way home and my car stopped. I don't know what's going on. I'm right over here on Collins. I was hoping you could come get me."

"You know I got you. What you gonna do with your car?"

"The tow truck is going to take it to the car dealership."

"Okay, well you know you can ride with me and Darien to the party."

"Thanks! Maybe I'll do that. But come get me, it's getting dark out here."

"I'm on the way," Angel said, getting in her car.

Darien was pacing the marble foyer looking at his watch every couple of minutes. He had been blowing up Angel's phone for the last hour. At first he thought maybe she had made another quick stop or had gotten held up in traffic, but now her phone was going straight to voicemail and Darien felt something was terribly wrong. He didn't want to think the worse, but he couldn't shake the despair that flooded his mind.

"Still no word from Angel?" Darien's driver Keaton asked, interrupting his thoughts.

"No. Come on, let's drive around. Maybe something happened to her car and her phone died so she can't call me," Darien said as they headed out.

Keaton drove to all the shopping areas they thought Angel might've stopped at. About 45 minutes into them riding around Darien spotted her Aston Martin parked on Collins Avenue.

"Pull over, there go Angel's car," Darien directed. When they got close to her vehicle, Darien jumped out the back of the Rolls Royce and he immediately noticed Angel's iPhone under the car and her purse was still located inside. "Fuck!" he yelled out banging his fist on the hood of the car.

"What you wanna do, boss?" Keaton questioned.

Darien stood by Angel's car in deep thought. He was biting down on his bottom lip, balling his fist. He was ready to jab his entire arm through the glass window, but fought against it. Darien felt he was going to suffocate in his anger. Part of him wanted to call the police, but he knew this wasn't an attempted robbery gone wrong or some random act of crime. In his heart Darien knew exactly what this was... revenge. He had put the woman that he was going to ask to spend the rest of his life with tonight, in jeopardy and his worse fear was that it was too late to make it right.

Angel could hear what sounded like a herd of ponies click clacking on pavement. The noise seemed to be echoing which made her body feel as if it was vibrating. The uncertainty of it all was scarier than how she actually got there. Angel remembered that one minute Taren was flagging her down and the next she was being thrown in the back of a black van.

Fuck! I hope Taren is okay. Is she here with me or did they already kill her? Please don't let Taren be dead. But who would want to hurt her and who would want to kidnap me? Angel thought to herself trying to understand what the hell was going on.

"Take off the blindfold," Angel heard a man say. She immediately started looking around, wanting to take in her surroundings. She was being held in a huge empty warehouse that only had a large steel table in the center. The next thing Angel zoomed in on was more than a half dozen men dressed in black holding guns, all but one man. He was dressed in an all black suit with two men standing on both sides of him. It wasn't until he stepped into the light that Angel finally made eye contact with the man.

"What's your name young lady," Nico asked politely.

"Motherfucker, you had your goons kidnap me and drag me down to this dungeon. So you know what the fuck my name is!" Angel spat, trying to wiggle her way out of the grasp of the two men holding her.

"Calm it down," one of the men shouted, squeezing Angel's arm tighter.

"Wait, wait wait," Nico ordered, holding his hand up. The men backed down and released Angel from their grasp. "No need to get upset, young lady." Nico smiled.

"No need to get upset? You can't be serious! You have your men drag and blindfold me then bring me to this dump on my birthday. Now you wanna stand there and tell me I have no reason to be upset. Get the fuck outta here. Upset is an understatement. And what about my friend Taren, is she okay? She's not dead is she?" Angel wanted to know. "And can you please take these tight ass handcuffs off my wrist?" she snapped.

Nico nodded his head, signaling for his men to oblige Angel's request. Angel felt a small sense of freedom and stretched her arms before pulling her sweated out hair from her face, putting it in a high bun.

"Nobody is dead... yet," Nico stated. "But that can all change very quickly," he made clear, coming closer. Once Nico was standing in front of Angel his eyes widened in disbelief. It was as if he had seen a ghost.

"Why the hell are you looking at me like that?" Angel barked, as an eerie feeling seem to smack her in the face.

"You look exactly like a woman I used to know."

"So fuckin' what. They say everyone has a twin right," Angel retorted.

"How old are you? You can't be any more than 20, 21. What is your mother's name?"

"Get the fuck away from me you creep before I spit in your face!" Angel growled, putting her head down, no longer wanting to look at Nico's face. That's when Nico saw it. A small teardrop shaped birthmark on the back of Angel's neck. Nico placed his hand on the back of his neck because he had the exact birthmark in the same location.

"Lisa, your mother's name is Lisa."

Angel's body seemed to freeze when Nico said her mother's name. She had never seen her mother a day in her life except from pictures.

There was no denying they practically looked like twins. A day never went by when Angel's mother didn't cross her mind and it was painful to hear her name.

"How do you know my mother and what sort of sick game are you playing?" Angel asked, staring deeply into Nico's dark eyes.

"Because you're my...." Before Nico could complete his sentence, he and his men were ambushed with a hail of bullets. Without hesitation, Nico threw his body over Angel's trying to protect her from the onslaught of gunshots.

Nico's small army of men began returning fire and it seemed like an all out war had begun within a matter of seconds. With the amount of gunfire ripping through the building it would be a miracle if anyone made it out alive.

Female Hustler Part 2
Coming Soon...

All I See Is The Money...

Female 2 Hustler

A Novel

JOY DEJA KING

A KING PRODUCTION

DRAKE

A NOVEL

JOY DEJA KING
AND CHRIS BOOKER

Prologue

"Push! Push!" the doctor directed Kim, as he held the top of the baby's head, hoping this would be the final push that would bring a new life into the world.

The hospital's delivery room was packed with both Kim and Drake's family, and although the large crowd irritated Drake, he still managed to video record the birth of his son. After four hours of labor, Kim gave birth to a 6.5-pound baby boy, whom they already named Derrick Jamal Henson Jr. Drake couldn't help but to shed a few tears of joy at the new addition to his family, but the harsh reality of his son's safety quickly replaced his joy with anger.

Drake was nobody's angel and beyond his light brown eyes and charming smile, he was one of the most feared men in the city of Philadelphia, due to his street credentials. He put a lot of work in on the blocks of South Philly, where he grew up. He mainly pushed drugs and gambled, but from time to time he'd place well-known dealers into the trunk of his car and hold them for ransom, according to how much that person was worth.

"I need everybody to leave the room for awhile," Drake told the people in the hospital room, wanting to share a private moment alone with Kim and his son.

The families took a few minutes saying their good-byes, before leaving. Kim and Drake sat alone in the room, rejoicing over the birth of baby Derrick. The only interruption was doctors coming in and out of the room, to check up on the baby, mainly because they were a little concerned about his breathing. The doctor informed Drake that he would run a few more tests to make sure the baby would be fine.

"So, what are you going to do?" Kim questioned Drake, while he was cradling the baby.

"Do about what?" he shot back, without lifting his head up. Drake knew what Kim was alluding to, but he had no interest in discussing it. Once Kim became pregnant, Drake agreed to leave the street life alone, if not completely then significantly cutting back, after their baby was born. They both feared if he didn't stop living that street life, he would land in the box. Drake felt he and jail were like night and day: they could never be together.

"You know what I'm talking about, Drake. Don't play stupid with me," Kim said, poking him in his head with her forefinger.

He smiled. "I gave you my word I was out of the game when you had our baby. Unless my eyes are deceiving me, I think what I'm holding in my arms is our son. Just give me a couple days to clean up the streets and then we can sit down and come up with a plan on how to invest the money we got."

Cleaning up the streets meant selling all the drugs he had and collecting the paper owed to him from his workers and guys he fronted weight to. All together there was about 100k due, not to mention the fact he had to appoint someone to take over his bread-winning crack houses and street corners that made him millions of dollars.

Drake's thoughts came to a halt when his phone started to ring. Sending the call straight to voicemail didn't help any, because it rang again. Right when he reached to turn the phone off, he noticed it was Peaches calling. If it were anybody else, he probably would've declined, but Peaches wasn't just anybody.

"Yo," he answered, shifting the baby to his other arm, while trying to avoid Kim's eyes cutting over at him.

"He knows! He knows everything!" Peaches yelled, with terror in her voice.

Peaches wasn't getting good reception out in the woods, where Villain had left her for dead, so the words Drake was hearing were broken up. All he understood was "Villain knows!" That was enough to get his heart racing. His heart wasn't racing out of fear, but rather excitement.

In many ways, Villain and Drake were cut from the same cloth. They even both shared tattoos of several teardrops under their eyes. It seemed like gunplay was the only thing that turned Drake on—besides fucking—and when he could feel it in the air, murder was the only thing on his mind.

Drake hung up the phone and tried to call Peaches back to see if he could get better reception, but her phone went straight to voicemail. Damn! He thought to himself as he tried to call her back repeatedly and block out Kim's voice as she steadily asked him if everything was all right.

"Drake, what's wrong?"

"Nothing, I gotta go. I'll be back in a couple of hours," he said, handing Kim their son.

"How sweet! There's nothing like family!" said a voice coming from the direction of the door.

Not yet lifting his head up from his son to see who had entered the room, at first Drake thought it was a doctor, but once the sound of the familiar voice kicked in, Drake's heart began beating at an even more rapid pace. He turned to see Villain standing in the doorway, chewing on a straw and clutching what appeared to be a gun at his waist. Drake's first instinct was to reach for his own weapon, but remembering that he left it in the car made his insides burn. Surely, if he had his gun on him, there would have been a showdown right there in the hospital.

"Can I come in?" Villain asked, in an arrogant tone, as he made his way over to the visitors' chairs. "Let me start off by saying congratulations on having a bastard child."

Villain's remarks made Drake's jaw flutter continuously from fury. Sensing shit was about to go left, Kim attempted to get out of the bed with her baby to leave the room, but before her feet could hit the floor, Villain pulled out a .50 Caliber Desert Eagle and placed it on his lap. The gun was so enormous that Drake could damn near read off the serial number on the slide. Kim looked at the nurse's button and was tempted to press it.

"Push the button and I'll kill all three of y'all. Scream and I'ma kill all three of y'all. Bitch," Villian paused, making sure the words sunk in, "if you even blink the wrong way, I'ma kill all three of y'all."

"What the fuck you want?" Drake asked, still trying to be firm in his speech.

"You know, at first, I thought about getting my money back and then killin' you, for setting my brother up wit' those bitches you got working for you. But on my way here I just said, 'Fuck the money!' I just wanna kill the nigga."

Deep down inside, Drake wanted to ask for his life to be spared, but his pride wouldn't allow it. Not even the fact that his newborn son was in the room could make Drake beg to stay alive, which made Villain even more eager to lullaby his ass into a permanent sleep.

Villain wanted to see the fear in his eyes before he pulled the trigger, but Drake was a G, and was bound to play that role 'til he kissed death.

Chapter 1

TWO MONTHS EARLIER

The sounds of gunshots filled the air as the day was winding down at the Last Shot Gun Range, which for some reason seemed crowded for a Sunday. Sunday was the day Drake and Peaches took off to tighten up on their shooting. Plus, there was something about firing a gun that relieved stress for the both of them after a long week. It was at this very range nine months ago that Drake and Peaches met for the first time. The mutual feeling they shared for guns is what brought them together, and the ambition to take over the world is what made them closer.

In booth five, Peaches stood there wearing a pair of skintight, light-blue jeans, a white tank top, and a pair of designer six-inch heels that seemed much better suited for a nightclub. Over her eyes was a pair of Bvlgari shield pink gold with gloss black sunglasses. Her jet-black curls framed her flawless deep chocolate skin, and she was clutching a .45 ACP, firing at her target.

"Did you take care of what I asked you to?" Drake asked, sliding up behind her while she fired at the target.

"Yeah. I called Ralph, and he said everything was a go for next Thursday. I told him that you would call him Tuesday."

"What about you? Are you ready for this?" Drake asked, lowering her weapon and turning her to face him.

This was a big sting for a lot of money, and Drake couldn't afford to mess this up. It could cost them their lives if something was to go wrong.

Peaches had set plenty of niggas up for the take-down, and she was good at what she did, but Tazz wasn't the one you get caught slippin' with. Tazz was the type to kill you in front of a hundred people, drag your body to the middle of the street, stand on top of it like he was King Kong, and dare anyone to say anything. It was rumored that he killed his father when he was eight years old because his dad used to beat up on his mom. He never shed a tear on the day of the funeral. People really thought he was possessed by the devil.

The one thing about Tazz was that he had money stacked to the ceiling. His dope was so pure that people thought he manufactured it himself. If everything worked out as planned, the take on this robbery would be in the millions.

"You know we still got some homework to do," Drake continued. "I want you to go buy a couple of burn-out cell phones, and go buy something super sexy for the bedroom." He wrapped his arms around her waist and pressed his dick up against her ass.

Although Drake had a main chick named Kim, Peaches had grabbed a piece of his heart over time, but they had an understanding. Peaches could fuck whomever she wanted as long as Drake and Kim stayed together. He had three simple rules for Peaches, and as long as these rules didn't get violated he would never turn his back on her:

Rule number one was that besides her, Drake came first. Rule number two was that Drake was the only one who went inside of her raw; i.e. without a condom, and that included that his dick was the only one she sucked. The third rule was that Peaches couldn't ever lie to him.

He figured that if she would lie then she'd cheat, and if she cheated, she'd steal. None of the three were acceptable, and none of it really mattered, because all Peaches wanted to do was be with Drake. She realized he was with her most of the time, so she felt confident that she was actually number one. Peaches couldn't even bring herself to give up the pussy to anybody other than Drake anyway.

"What about Ralph?" Peaches asked in a concerned manner. "I really don't trust dat muthafucker. He knows I'm ya girl, but he keeps running dat old ass bullshit game on me like I'm suppose to bite."

"Ralph ain't nothin', but a puppet. After the score, I'll take care of him. Just play it cool in the meantime, and show da nigga a titty every now and again to keep him happy," Drake whispered in her ear jokingly, making her laugh thinking that's all it took to get Ralph excited.

A police car had been sitting on the corner of 23rd Street near Tasker Avenue for the past two days, slowing up a lot of money for Cindy. This street was her gold mine because every crack-head from 32nd Street to 16th Street came and copped there, including a few out-of-towners who preferred to buy a little weight. Twenty-third Street alone pulled in about fifteen thousand a shift, with three shifts a day. It was hard for smokers to resist the best coke in the city, and with that, a lot of jealousy was raised from the dead.

Cindy literally took over South Philly in the early 2000s, and had no plans on loosening up her grip when she inherited the drug business from her father, Mark, after he was killed in front of her during a home invasion. Niggas in the hood respected her G when she rocked to sleep the same dudes who shot Mark, leaving a small trail of unsolved homicides in her path. People in the hood had love for Mark, and when they finally got a chance to meet Cindy, they could see a lot of Mark in her. The old saying, "A woman is a reflection of her man," which in this case meant Cindy's father was true, and everybody felt the same way, even Chris, a relentless rival. Cindy inherited more than just the drug business from her father. She also inherited his beef/competition.

Cindy pulled up to 23rd Street in a silver, tricked out Range Rover. She couldn't help but, notice the cop car sitting on the corner, so she called Lil' Rick, one of the three workers she had on this shift. Before she could dial the number, Rick came out of a house on the block.

Cindy was no stranger to the streets, so when she stepped out of the truck, a couple of kids that were playing on the sidewalk spoke to her as she walked towards Rick. The sun glistened off of her caramel complexion, as she walked on the sidewalk with her Jeffrey Campbell's Popp sneakers. The kick-ass shoes featured gold hardware lace, black velcro buckles, gold lettering, and hot pink lining with a zip closure on the side. She paired the look with some cutoff jean shorts, a tank top and her hair was slicked back in a ballerina bun. Although she was casually dressed, her diamond studs, expensive purse that hung on her shoulder, and iced out wrist let you know Cindy's coins were very long.

"The block is hot right now," Rick said, meeting her at the mom and pop store on the corner. "The nigga, Chris, been sending shooters through here every day for three days straight, trying to rob the workers. My man, P., that works the night shift shot one of them last night."

"What about the cops?" Cindy inquired, seeing the lack of money being made.

"At first they just passed through when they got a report of gunshots being fired, but ever since last night one cop car just sits on the corner all day. The guy that P. shot almost bled to death and it drew a big crowd. The shit was all over the news and everything."

Even though the cops were sitting on the corner, crack-heads were still bold enough to come down the street, so the workers were bold enough to make a few sales behind parked cars. Money was being made, but it had slowed down considerably.

Cindy was feeling some type of way that business wasn't booming. Although 23rd Street was her main strip, it wasn't her only one. Because it was an established spot, she was optimistic things would pick back up soon. But now that Chris came out of his shell, it was about time that Cindy made the streets remember who she was and the consequences that came with crossing her.

"Look, I want everybody to fall back for a couple of days so the heat can cool down. I don't want anybody selling a single rock out here. We'll open up shop in a couple of days," she explained to Rick. "We got to get these guys off the corner," she said, nodding in the direction of the cop car.

Cindy jumped back into her truck, and before she pulled off, she called D-Rock, an old-timer who rolled with her dad when he was alive. D-Rock was a legend in the hood, and everybody respected him mainly because he still put in work at the age of fifty. He wasn't a hit man for Cindy, but rather an advisor and a friend that she could talk to about almost anything. After her dad died, D-Rock basically raised her from the age of 17. Despite the fact that Cindy was one of the biggest drug dealers in the city, D-Rock had love for her and became a father figure in her life.

..e small crew Tazz kept around him was about their
..usiness when it came to gunplay, Drake thought to him-
elf after noticing two out of five men that surrounded
Tazz in front of the club he owned.

Drake had been following Tazz around for the past
two days, trying to see any patterns in his movements
that could be useful. There wasn't anything unusual or
useful, and even though Drake already knew where Tazz
lived, he hadn't been home in two days.

Villain was the first person Drake noticed. He was
sitting on the hood of a BMW 7 Series Sedan with Tazz.
He knew Villain from a couple years back. They were
fuckin' the same chick at one point, and she used to tell
Drake all about how crazy Villain was and who the latest
victim was that he shot. It seemed like every time Drake
went to fuck the broad, she had a new story about the
dude.

Drake's phone began to vibrate with an incom-
ing call. It was Kim. He thought about answering it, but
he was stalking his prey at the moment and wanted no
interruptions. He had to stay focused. If Drake made
the wrong move and Tazz had any idea that he was two
blocks away watching him, Tazz would have somebody
come light the car up with bullets before he got a chance
to pull off. Besides, Drake was about to head home in a
couple of hours because being outside for two days without a shower and a good night's sleep could take a toll on
anybody.

The second person he noticed in the crew was Ice.
Drake knew Ice from the county jail about a year back.
Ice was fighting a double homicide while Drake was
fighting an attempted murder charge. Everyone knew

that Ice killed the people he was locked up for, but nobody was willing to take the chance on testifying against him. Drake beat his case before Ice did, so when he got released from county that was the last time he saw him until now. From the looks of things, Ice beat his case, too.

Drake's phone started vibrating again. This time it was Ralph, and this wasn't a call he could ignore. Looking around his car at empty potato chip bags and empty soda cans, he found his phone under the trash. "Yo, holla at ya boy."

"What's good, Drake? Can you meet me right now?"

"Give me the place," Drake said, starting his car with intentions on leaving.

"The McDonald's on Broad Street, in two hours," Ralph said, then hung up the phone.

Just when Drake was about to pull off, he saw a dark-colored Benz pull up in front of the club, and out jumped a woman with a bag in her hand. Instead of pulling off, Drake grabbed the binoculars to get a better look at what was going on. The bag looked like it had some weight to it. Tazz quickly grabbed the bag from her and took it into the club.

Drake pulled off, wondering what could be in the bag. He didn't know if it was money, drugs, or just nothing at all, but for now it was time to get home, take a shower, and then go meet up with Ralph. Sleep was not an option today; and if money were on the line, Drake would always push it to the limit.

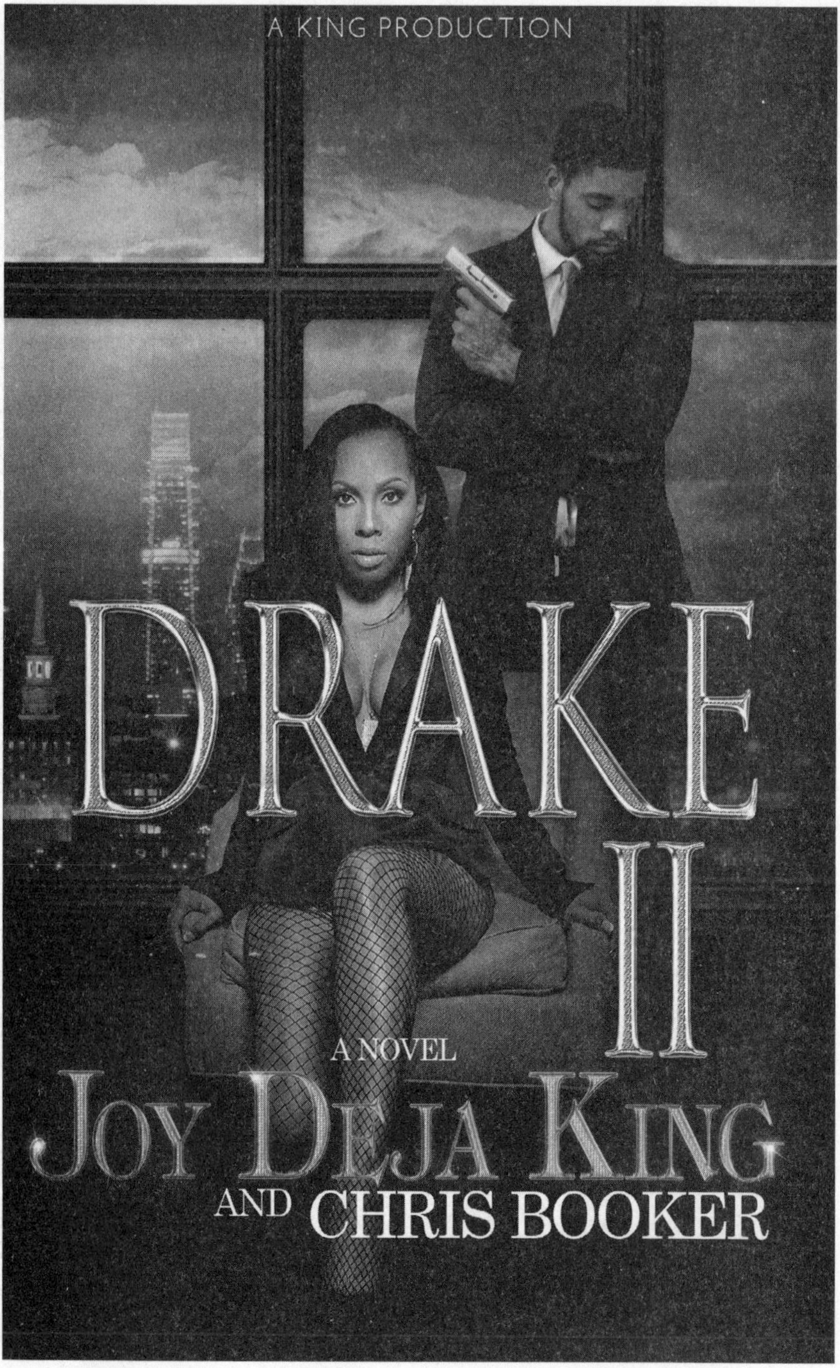
A KING PRODUCTION
DRAKE
II
A NOVEL
JOY DEJA KING
AND CHRIS BOOKER

A KING PRODUCTION

Power

NO ONE MAN SHOULD HAVE ALL THAT POWER...BUT THERE WERE TWO

JOY DEJA KING

Chapter 1
UNDERGROUND KING

Alex stepped into his attorney's office to discuss what was always his number one priority...business. When he sat down their eyes locked and there was complete silence for the first few seconds. This was Alex's way of setting the tone of the meeting. His silence spoke volumes. This might've been his attorney's office but he was the head nigga in charge and nothing got started until he decided it was time to speak. Alex felt this approach was necessary. You see, after all these years of them doing business, attorney George Lofton still wasn't used to dealing with a man like Alex; a dirt-poor kid who could've easily died in the projects he was born in, but instead had made millions. It wasn't done the ski mask way but it was still illegal.

They'd first met when Alex was a sixteen-year-old kid growing up in TechWood Homes, a housing project in Atlanta. Alex and his best friend, Deion, had been arrested because the principal found 32 crack vials in Alex's book bag. Another kid had tipped the principal off and the principal subsequently called the police. Alex and Deion were arrested and suspended from school. His mother called George, who had the charges against them dismissed, and they were allowed to go back to school. But that wasn't the last time he would use George. He was arrested at twenty-two for attempted murder, and for trafficking cocaine a year later. Alex was acquitted on both charges. George Lofton later became known as the best trial attorney in Atlanta, but Alex had also become the best at what he did. And since it was Alex's money that kept Mr. Lofton in designer suits, million dollar homes and foreign cars, he believed he called the shots, and dared his attorney to tell him otherwise.

Alex noticed that what seemed like a long period of silence made Mr. Lofton feel uncomfortable, which he liked. Out of habit, in order to camouflage the discomfort, his attorney always kept bottled water within arm's reach. He would cough, take a swig, and lean back in his chair, raising his eyebrows a little, trying to give a look of certainty, though he wasn't completely confident at all in Alex's presence. The reason was because Alex did what many had thought would be impossible, especially men like George Lofton. He had gone from a knucklehead, low-level drug dealer to an underground king and an unstoppable respected criminal boss.

Before finally speaking, Alex gave an intense stare into George Lofton's piercing eyes. They were not only the bluest he had ever seen, but also some of the most calculating. The latter is what Alex found so compelling. A calculating attorney working on his behalf could almost guarantee a get out of jail free card for the duration of his criminal career.

"Have you thought over what we briefly discussed the other day?" Alex asked his attorney, finally breaking the silence.

"Yes I have, but I want to make sure I understand you correctly. You want to give me six hundred thousand to represent you or your friend Deion if you are ever arrested and have to stand trial again in the future?"

Alex assumed he had already made himself clear based on their previous conversations and was annoyed by what he now considered a repetitive question. "George, you know I don't like repeating myself. That's exactly what I'm saying. Are we clear?"

"So this is an unofficial retainer."

"Yes, you can call it that."

George stood and closed the blinds then walked over to the door that led to the reception area. He turned the deadbolt so they wouldn't be disturbed. George sat back behind the desk. "You know that if you and your friend Deion are ever on the same case that I can't represent the both of you."

"I know that."

"So what do you propose I do if that was ever to happen?"

"You would get him the next best attorney in Atlanta," Alex said without hesitation. Deion was Alex's best friend—had been since the first grade. They were now business partners, but the core of their bond was built on that friendship, and because of that Alex would always look out for Deion's best interest.

"That's all I need to know."

Alex clasped his hands and stared at the ceiling for a moment, thinking that maybe it was a bad idea bringing the money to George. Maybe he should have just put it somewhere safe only known to him and his mom. He quickly dismissed his concerns.

"Okay. Where's the money?" Alex presented George with two leather briefcases. He opened the first one and was glad to see that it was all hundred-dollar bills. When he closed the briefcase he asked, "There is no need to count this is there?"

"You can count it if you want, but it's all there."

George took another swig of water. The cash made him nervous. He planned to take it directly to one of his bank safe deposit boxes. The two men stood. Alex was a foot taller than George; he had flawless mahogany skin, a deep brown with a bit of a red tint, broad shoulders, very large hands, and a goatee. He was a man's man. With such a powerful physical appearance, Alex kept his style very low-key. His only display of wealth was a pricey diamond watch that his best friend and partner Deion had bought him for his birthday.

"I'll take good care of this, and you," his attorney said, extending his hand to Alex.

"With this type of money, I know you will," Alex stated without flinching. Alex gave one last lingering stare into his attorney's piercing eyes. "We do have a clear understanding...correct?"

"Of course. I've never let you down and I never will. That, I promise you." The men shook hands and

Alex made his exit with the same coolness as his entrance.

With Alex embarking on a new, potentially dangerous business venture, he wanted to make sure that he had all his bases covered. The higher up he seemed to go on the totem pole, the costlier his problems became. But Alex welcomed new challenges because he had no intention of ever being a nickel and dime nigga again.

Order Form

A King Production
P.O. Box 912
Collierville, TN 38027
www.joydejaking.com
www.twitter.com/joydejaking

Name: _____

Address: _____

City/State: _____

Zip: _____

QUANTITY	TITLES	PRICE	TOTAL
____	Bitch	$15.00	_____
____	Bitch Reloaded	$15.00	_____
____	The Bitch Is Back	$15.00	_____
____	Queen Bitch	$15.00	_____
____	Last Bitch Standing	$15.00	_____
____	Superstar	$15.00	_____
____	Ride Wit' Me	$12.00	_____
____	Stackin' Paper	$15.00	_____
____	Trife Life To Lavish	$15.00	_____
____	Trife Life To Lavish II	$15.00	_____
____	Stackin' Paper II	$15.00	_____
____	Rich or Famous	$15.00	_____
____	Rich or Famous Part 2	$15.00	_____
____	Bitch A New Beginning	$15.00	_____
____	Mafia Princess Part 1	$15.00	_____
____	Mafia Princess Part 2	$15.00	_____
____	Mafia Princess Part 3	$15.00	_____
____	Mafia Princess Part 4	$15.00	_____
____	Mafia Princess Part 5	$15.00	_____
____	Boss Bitch	$15.00	_____
____	Baller Bitches Vol. 1	$15.00	_____
____	Baller Bitches Vol. 2	$15.00	_____
____	Baller Bitches Vol. 3	$15.00	_____
____	Bad Bitch	$15.00	_____
____	Still The Baddest Bitch	$15.00	_____
____	Power	$15.00	_____
____	Power Part 2	$15.00	_____
____	Drake	$15.00	_____
____	Drake Part 2	$15.00	_____
____	Female Hustler	$15.00	_____
____	Princess Fever "Birthday Bash"	$9.99	_____

Shipping/Handling (Via Priority Mail) $6.50 1-2 Books, $8.95 3-4 Books add
$1.95 for ea. Additional book.

Total: $_____ FORMS OF ACCEPTED PAYMENTS: Certified or government
issued checks and money Orders, all mail in orders take 5-7 Business days to be delivered